PRAYERS OF DELIVERANCE

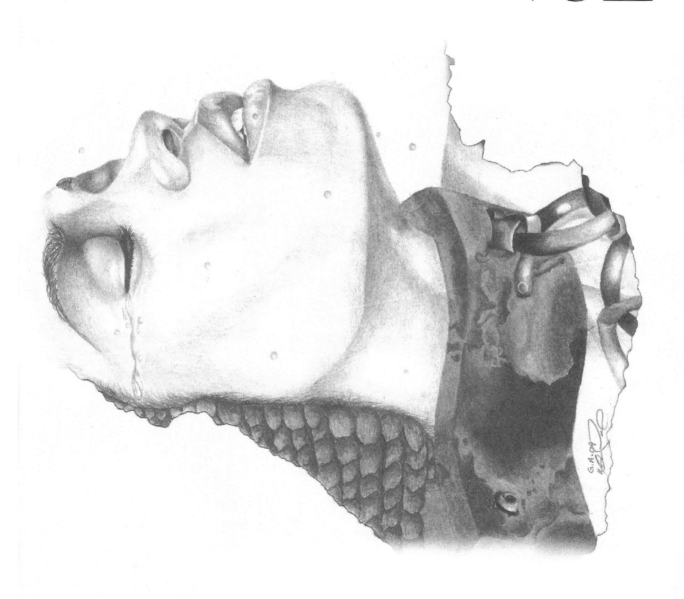

"Prayers of Deliverance"

All the stories are fictional. However, they may reflect on what you or someone you may know are going through in your life. Read their stories and know, that no matter what you are going through, God is always there and that Yeshua is going through them with you. Keep your trust and faith strong in Him no matter how much it may hurt within your heart and spirit. He hurts as well. You're never alone.

Bible scripture taken from the New King James version of the Holy Bible Printed by Thomas Nelson Inc. Copyright 1979, 1982,1994

DEDICATION

This book is dedicated to Viola Anderson/ Homeretta (Cookie) Gillespie/Francis Wade/Lydia Farrington/ Mary A. Peaks/ Stacey Christiana Anderson/ Nancy Wade/ Venice Samuels/Ena Freeman/ Tiffany (T-Bone) Tarver/Chrystal Christian and to all the young girls and young women all around the world who are going through the fire of life. Know this, that God our Savior, our Healer and our Deliverer, will never leave you alone nor lonely. He is there with all of you. He feels your pain and He feels your tears of sorrow. So, please don't give up on our Father nor our Savior Yeshua. Stand strong in your faith and know that you are no one's property. You are God's vessel. Stay encouraged my daughters and sisters in Christ.

This book is for you Lydia Lucille Samuels. R.I.C. (Rest In Christ). I love you Cille.

You Are

You are mothers, sisters, daughters, nieces, aunts, grandmothers, wives. Whoever you may be, know that you are meant to be loved, respected and honored by all mankind. Mankind is a word that has very little meaning these days. For, you are not only the bearer of life, but a precious vessel created by the loving hands of God Himself. You are Mary: The bearer of our Lord and Savior. You are Sarah: The mother of many nations. You are Esther: The star, a chosen Queen of God. You are Naomi: A woman of God's delight. You are Priscilla: An instructed Christian of God. You are Bashemath: Her spiritual beauty was that of the sweet scent of frankincense and myrrh; and a daughter of Solomon. You are Bathsheba: The bearer of wisdom, King Solomon. You are Eve: The mother of all mankind. Without the love and compassion of our Heavenly Father, mankind could not exist without woman. Understand that not all women feel that they are a part of this tree of God's creation. But you are. Mankind must acknowledge the gift that God has given him in the beginning. And if we say we love God and ourselves, then we must love woman as ourselves, as God loves us. They were created from us. Our minds, our bodies, our souls, our spirit. To bring harm upon them, we bring harm upon ourselves. We as mankind must recognize their existence as God has recognized ours. We must give them the love, compassion, understanding, patience, humbleness, strength and courage that our Heavenly Father granted us on the day He created us. Withstanding all trials and tribulations of life, with the love of Yeshua in our hearts, our minds, our souls and our spirits.

"Prayers of Deliverance" consist of spirit filled stories of young girls and women, from around the world and of different cultures, seeking God's deliverance from their trials and tribulations of life. Read, as they cry out to be delivered from their pains and sufferings. Read, as God answers to their prayers, not just in scripture, but as a loving and compassionate Father. I hope you will be touched in your heart and spirit by reading their stories and know that God will never leave you nor forsake you.

"Weeping may endure for a night. But joy will come in the morning."

Dear God;

I am so lost and so afraid right now. I'm just 15 years old and I'm pregnant. I dare not tell my parents. My dad had big hopes for me. I'm an A+ student in school and my mom and dad have plans for me to go to school to become a doctor, because I love helping people. My parents and I go to church every Sunday, and I'm the leader of our Vacation Bible School during the summer. My bible school-teacher calls on me to lead the class in prayer and to end it in prayer. She even looks to me to help the other kids with their Sunday school lesson. One day while we were at the Vacation Bible School picnic, I met this boy. His name is Randle. He seemed to be a very nice boy. His father is the minister of our church. We would take walks to the pond, just behind the church and quote bible scripture to each other, to see who's the smartest. We would even sometimes act out the rolls of people of the bible. Like one time he pretended to be Moses. He would pick up a stick off the ground and pretend he was parting the pond, which would be the Red Sea. I would pretend to be the woman who touched the helm of Jesus's garment so that I would be healed. On the last day of Vacation Bible School, our teacher took the class on a field trip to the petting zoo. There, they had a big lake and a lot of animals. Me and Randle snuck away down by the lake. This time he pretended to be Abraham and I was Sarah. Randle said that we were husband and wife and that we had to kiss like husband and wife. So, I kissed him. Then Randle started to touch my private parts. That's what my mom called them. I told him to stop, but he said that is how Abraham became the father of many nations. So, I told him it was ok. I don't think I need to say anything else God, because I think You already know what happened after that. Well, two months before regular school started, I woke up that morning with a belly ache. I ran to the bathroom and threw up in the toilet. My mom came in the bathroom and asked me what was wrong. I told her that I had a belly ache, but I would be ok to go to school.

While in Miss Richards class, I got sick again and ran out of the classroom and straight to the restroom and threw up again. My teacher came in and asked me if I was ok. I told her that it must have been something that I ate. She asked if I wanted her to call my parents. I told her no and that I would be ok. Just then the school bell rang for recess. After I washed my face, I went to the library and got on the computer to see if I could find out what made me feel sick. After being there for at least an hour, I found out why I was feeling so sick. I am pregnant. I sat there for a very long time, not knowing what to do or what to say. I finally got up and not only walked out the library, but also school. No one seemed to pay any attention to me as I walked out and started walking home. Trying to figure out what I am going to tell my mom and dad. I could run away, but that would hurt them even more. But I can't tell them. I feel that I was betrayed by Randle. He took my life from me. But I also know that it was wrong. Oh, Lord; please help me. Please God. Tell me what to do because I don't know what to do. I am so, so lost right now.

        This is Your Daughter

My Sweet, Loving Daughter;

I am the Good Shepherd. The good shepherd gives His life for the sheep. But, a hireling, he who is not the shepherd, one who does not own the sheep, sees the wolf coming and leaves the sheep and flees; and the wolf catches the sheep and scatters them. The hireling flees because he is the hireling and does not care about the sheep; and I know My sheep; and am known by My own. As the Father knows Me, even so I know the Father, and I lay down My life for the sheep. And other sheep I have which are not of this fold, them also I must bring; and they will hear My voice and there will be one flock and one shepherd. Therefore, My Father loves Me because I lay down My life that I may take it again. No one takes it from Me, but I lay it down of Myself. I have power to lay it down and I have power to take it again. This command I have received from My Father. Always know this My child; My sheep hear My voice and I know them, and they follow Me as you have always followed Me. And I give them eternal life, and they shall never perish; neither shall anyone snatch them out of My hand. You are My little sheep and I will always be your Shepherd. You must be truthful with your parents as you are with Me. They will not forsake you. For they too, are my sheep. I will be with you my child rather you are amongst the wolves or in the midst there of.

My Heavenly Father;

I've lived in the slums of India all my life. My mother was a prostitute and I never knew who my father was. Two weeks ago, a policeman saw me on the streets and told me that I needed to come with him to the hospital. I asked him why. He told me that my mother was in there and that she was dying. So, I went with him. When we got to her room, she looked at me and told me that I looked like my father. And that she hated my father for raping her. That makes me a product of a rape. She told me that she gave birth to me while looking for food in the dump fields of Calcutta. When I was 10 years old, I could remember that my mother sold me to this man for 30 rupees. He seemed to be a very nice man. He owned 4 businesses and was well known through-out the slums, even though he didn't stay there. His driver drove us to his house. It looked like a palace. So very beautiful. He had servants and butlers. But there was this one old lady who took care of the house and all of his guest. When I got out of the car, the old lady came up to the man and greeted him. I didn't have any luggage, except for this dirty old bag that I carried an old blue dress I found in the garbage and my only pair of sandals that were worn out and the straps were broken. Standing there, the man told the old lady to take my bag and show me to my room. She took my bag and grabbed my hand and said, "Come with me child." We walked in the house and, WOW! It was beautiful! As we walked up the long flight of stairs, I could see all the different kind of paintings on the walls and the beautiful chandeliers hanging from the ceiling with every 10 steps we took. They lit up the house so bright it could be daylight inside. When we reached the top of the stairs, there was this long hallway where the floor looked as clear as glass and the walls were as white as snow. I was so amazed at the beauty of this house. It was like I was living the life of a lost princess. When we reached the third door down, the old lady opened the door and walked in. She turned and looked at me and said, "Come child. Don't be afraid. This is your new home now." When I walked in, it was like walking into a fairy tale. Something like Sleeping Beauty or even Cinderella. The room was huge. There was this very big bed with white lace all around it, big fluffy pillows, too many for me to count at one time. In front of the bed was something that looked like a pool. Next to it stood two more old women with towels as white as the clouds in the sky. One of them walked up to me and said, "Come child so we can bathe you." I thought to myself, "WOW!" This is not a pool, but a bathtub. It was full of bubbles and it smelled so good. A smell much different than that of the smells of the garbage dumps. While the ladies were bathing me, a knock came at the door and a voice spoke out, "Dinner in 15 minutes." As the women took me out of the tub, dried me off, then quickly dressed me and fixed my hair. As we were walking out, there was this very large mirror behind the door. I stopped for a moment just to take a look at myself. I couldn't believe that was me I was looking at. "Let's go child. We can't keep master waiting," one lady said. As we headed down the stairs, and through these two gigantic doors, I saw a table full of food. It was set as a table meant for a king. And the food smelled so good. My stomach started growling with hunger pains. A butler escorted me to a chair at one end of the table and pulled the chair out and told me to have a seat. When I sat down, I was ready to eat. I reached for a piece of bread, when the butler told me to wait for his master to enter the room. Just then, the man walked in the room. He was dressed like a king, even though he wasn't. He wasn't that tall. Kind of short. He walked up to me and said, "Welcome to my home." Then he turned and walked to his seat as a butler pulled his chair out for him to be seated. Once he sat down, the butler that was standing by me said, "You can eat now child." I started eating like there was no tomorrow. The butler told me to slow down and chew my food before I get sick. As I looked up, I saw that the man was watching me as I ate. "Are you enjoying your meal?" he asked me. All I could do was nod my head in delight because my belly was full. So full, I started to fall asleep at the table. He called for the old lady to take me upstairs to get me ready for bed. When we got to the room, the old lady took off my clothes and put this white sleeping gown on me, put me in bed, kissed me on the forehead and told me to have sweet dreams. It didn't take long for me to fall asleep. But I was awaken by the touch of these very rough hands. I thought I was dreaming, having a nightmare, until I opened my eyes and saw the man in my bed with me and he was rubbing his hands all over my body. I asked him what he was doing. He didn't say a word. He just kept rubbing his hands all over me. As I pushed his hands away, he grabbed my hands and said that I belong to him. That I was bought and paid for and that he could do with me as he pleases. He took his tie off from around his neck and tied my hands to the bed. I cried to him and begged him to stop. He then took off his shirt and then his pants. I was about to scream. That's when he pulled a knife out of his pocket and said that if I screamed that he would cut my throat and throw my body right back in the dump fields where he bought me. Then he put one of his hands up my gown and ripped off my panties. He then ripped off my gown. As I laid there naked Lord, this man got on top of me. I felt a pain that I have never felt before in my entire life. Lord, that man who I trusted, hurt me so very bad. When he was done, he told me to get out the bed and go clean the blood off of me and not to get none on his floor. Lord, I couldn't move, I was in so much pain. This went on for about 4 years. He even paid a doctor to come and check me out in case I got pregnant. By the time I turned 18 years old, I became a play toy for his friends and his business partners. By age 25 I was prostituting for him. Father, oh my Father. How long will I have to endure this pain? I want to kill myself. But, I can't. Please Father God, in the name of Jesus, deliver me from this hell that I am in. Don't let my life end the way as my own mother. Please take my life. Please.

My Daughter, My child;

Let not your heart be troubled. You believe in God, believe also in Me. In My Father's house are many mansions. If it were not so, I would have told you. I go to prepare a place for you. A place where you will never be alone nor lonely. A place where no one will ever harm you again. And if I go and prepare a place for you, I will come again and receive you to Myself; that where I am, there you may be also. And where I go you know, and the way, you know. But, until that time of my return, I need for you to go out into the world and be a living testimony of My word and teach others that they may know of My undying love; to the saved as well as the sinner. So, be strong My daughter. I will be returning soon for you and all My daughters who remain faithful in Me and My Father. I love you my child.

Dear Lord;

As far back as I can remember as a child, my mom and dad would wake me and my two sisters up every Sunday morning for breakfast before we headed out for Sunday school. Mom would be in the kitchen making pancakes, while dad sat in the living room reading the Sunday paper. The sports section as usual. I was the oldest of the three of us, which meant I had the responsibility of getting my sisters ready for church. Kelly, the youngest, was always glued to her Sunday school lesson. She was our dad's little preacher. Maggie was always glued to the mirror in the bathroom. At the age of thirteen, Maggie saw herself as the next Miss Universe. Kelly, who's nine, wanted to grow up and be a Sunday school teacher like Mrs. Anderson. Me, at age 16, couldn't wait till church was over to go and hang out with my friends at the mall. Even on a school day, me and my friends couldn't wait for the bell to ring so that we could rush home, change our clothes and hook-up at the mall. One day after school, me and my friends went to the mall to buy some clothes for the summer, because it gets really hot and humid here in Chicago. We were planning to go to Oak Street Beach. While we were waiting for the bus, my mom called me on my cell phone. "Hey mom. What's up," I said. She was crying. She said that I needed to come home right away. I asked her what was wrong. She said it was my dad. I told my friends that I had to rush home. I jumped off the bus at the next stop and flagged down a taxi. "Take me to 5767 Humboldt Park Drive, and hurry please!" I shouted. When the cab pulled up to my house, I saw an ambulance and two police cars in front of my house. My mother and my sisters were on the front porch crying and hugging each other. The taxi man said, "That will be $22.50 lady." I don't know what I gave him, but I jumped out of the taxi and ran towards my mom. "Hey lady! You forgot your change!" he shouted. "Keep it!" I shouted back. I stopped at the bottom of the porch steps and my worst fears came to light. "Mom, where's dad," I asked her. She told Maggie to hold Kelly as she made her way down the steps. I looked in my mom's tear stained eyes as she grabbed me and hugged me. I pushed her away and shouted, "Where is my father!" "He's gone." "What do you mean he's gone," I asked her. "Your father is dead baby," she whispered. At that moment, I saw my whole world come crashing down around me. It was like life was snatched right out of my body. My mom tried to hug me, but I pulled away from her and ran. I have never felt so cold and so numb in all my life. For days after the funeral, I had that cold and numb feeling. Not one tear came out of my eyes. Days went by. Then months. And still not one tear. Mom was trying to find a job to take on the role of my dad. But things just weren't working out. Me and my sisters were always fighting. Mom was always yelling at us to do our housework. Things just weren't the same without my dad. Maggie stopped trying to look beautiful. Kelly stopped reading her bible lesson. We just stopped going to church all around. It got so bad around the house that my mom gave up totally. Not just her job, but on the three of us. So, I tried to do the best I could for my family. But it was so hard Lord. That is a job that no child should ever have to do. But my mom lost all hope. Then I started missing school, making sure that Maggie and Kelly went. Cleaning house while my mom stayed in bed all day feeling sorry for herself. I was doing the cooking, and the yard work. Even paying the bills. My mom was getting two checks a month. One from the state and one from my dad's pension. One day, my mom came out of her room and told me that she had to make a run. I asked her where she was going. She just walked right out the door without saying another word. While my mom was out and my sisters were playing in their room, our neighbor's son, Shorty, came by. He said he was sorry for me losing my dad. He asked me if I wanted to hang out with him and some of his friends at a daytime house party. I told him, "Sure, why not. Let me just go and get my sisters in order before we leave." He told me to wear a pair of jeans and a t-shirt. So, I ran up to my room and changed my clothes. As I was changing, Maggie came into my room and asked me where I was going. I told her that I was going across the street to Karen's house. She asked me why was I wearing mom's perfume. I told her that I will let her wear my favorite shoes to school if she didn't tell mom. She said, "Ok." As I left the house crossing the street to Karen's house, I turned around and saw Kelly looking out their bedroom window, seeing where I was going. When I reached Karen's house, I turned around and Kelly had left the window. Just then, I ran up the street where Shorty told me to meet him. Now, Shorty was 18 years old and a gangbanger, a Latin King. He was sitting in his dad's car, a black and blue 1983 Mustang. I walked up to the car and when Shorty saw me his eyes grew the size of lemons. "Wow! You look so hot!" he said. I replied thank you. "Are you ready to party?" he asked. "I am," with a look of relief on my face. It felt so good to get away from the house for a little while. While we were headed towards the party, all that was on my mind was having fun. Something I haven't done since my dad died. When we got up to the house where the party was being held, I could see a lot of cars and people standing outside drinking and smoking weed. The music was bumping from the inside so loud that I could feel the vibrations in the car. When Shorty parked the car, he got out and came over to my side; opened the door to let me out. When I got out, he closed the door and then took my hand and escorted me to the house as if I was his girlfriend. We walked in the house and there were maybe 6 girls and a room full of boys. I asked him where all the other girls are. He said that more was coming and that it was still early. We found a seat on the couch. I was a little nervous because an hour had gone by and no other girls showed up. That's when Shorty asked me if I wanted something to drink. I told him that I didn't drink alcohol. So, he said he would get a soda. Sitting there waiting for him to return, one of the girls that was there came over and sat next to me and asked me my name. That's when he returned. He handed me my soda and sat next to me. As I was drinking my soda, I was becoming a little sleep. "What's wrong? Are you ok?" Shorty asked me. I told him that I wanted to go home. He told me to relax and that he could take me upstairs to lie down for a few and he would be by my side until I felt better. So, I trusted him. As we walked upstairs, two girls were walking down-stairs giggling at me. I asked Shorty what was that all about. He said that they were just being silly, that's all. As we walked in the room, it was made up like a room for a little girl. "Whose room is this," I asked him. He said it was his friend's sister's room. He walked me over to the bed and laid me down. "Rest yourself. I'm going to be right here," he told me. I wondered off to sleep and the next thing I knew when I woke up was that my belly was hurting me so bad. I called out for Shorty, but he wasn't in the room. That's when I heard police sirens and gun shots. I got up off the bed and noticed that my clothes were wet. When I looked at myself, I had blood all on my pants and on the bed. I was terrified. I didn't know what to do. Then two police officers busted into the room with their guns in their hands. They told me to lie down on the floor. I was in tears. I asked them where Shorty was. They told me to shut my mouth and that I was in enough trouble as it is. They put the handcuffs on me and took me downstairs and put me in the police car. As we headed out the door, I saw Shorty standing in the living room. I called to him, but he walked away with another girl. I screamed for him to help me. One police officer asked him if he knew me. Shorty looked me straight into my eyes and told the officer that he has never seen me before in his life. The officer took me to the car, and they took me to the police station. Lord, I thought that was the worse day of my life. Being drugged then being raped. But it wasn't. At the police station, I asked if I could call my mom. They told me to wait until I was processed. When I did call, there was no answer. I tried two more times before the policeman told me to hang up the phone. I stayed in that cell for two days before a policewoman came and told me that I had a visitor. I was hoping that it was my mom. When she escorted me to the visiting room, there on the other side of the glass was my mom. I was so happy to see her. I cried telling her what really happened at that party. Then I asked her when I will be coming home. My mom looked at me and she didn't say one word. She didn't have no expression on her face. Not one. She didn't even ask if I was ok. But when she opened her mouth to speak, her words were words that I will never forget. "You left my babies in that house all by themselves. All alone so you could go to some damn party with some damn boy. You left my babies all by themselves. Anything could have happened. You knew how bad it is where we live with all the drugs and the gangs. But you had to go to a party and left my babies. I hope that boy was worth the sacrifice. Then my mom turned and called out to the policewoman. When I tried to explain, my mom looked at me with a look of hate; a look that cut right through my very soul. Before the policewoman opened the door, my mom came up close to the glass and said, "By the time you get out of here, we would be gone. We're moving. I can't afford for my babies to be around a gangbanger, a drug-dealer and a whore. Don't worry about trying to find us. You're on your own." When the door opened, my mom turned to the policewoman and told her that she was sorry, but she thought that I was her daughter and that she made a big mistake. With tears running down my face, I saw my life end. My mom didn't even look back as she walked out. I spent only one month in jail before they let me out. And within that month I come to find out that I was pregnant. I'm 28 now and have a beautiful little daughter. I'm working and going to school to make a better life for her. But my past still haunts me each and every day. I've made some bad decisions and terrible choices in my life. Please lead me back to the place where I belong. Please Lord cleanse my heart and spirit once again. Father, in the name of Jesus, keep my daughter as You have kept me.

My little girl;

You have been cleansed because you believed in Me. Abide in Me and I in you. As the branch cannot bear fruit of itself, unless it abides in the vine, neither can you, unless you abide in Me. I am the vine; you are the branches. He who abides in Me, and I in him (and her) bears much fruit. For without Me you can do nothing. If anyone does not abide in Me, he and she is cast out as a branch and is withered; and they gather them and throw them into the fire, and they are burned. If you abide in Me, my daughter, and My words abide in you, you will ask what you desire, and it shall be done for you. By this, My Father is glorified; that you bear much fruit, so you will be My Disciple. As the Father loved Me, I also have loved you; abide in My child.   Peace be unto you

Dear Lord;

I don't know if You can hear me or not. I guess You really don't have a reason to. But You're the only one I can talk to right now. I have no one else to turn to. My mom died 2 years ago, and my dad put me out the house because he said I was a troublemaker. Ever since my mom died, my dad has been drinking a lot. He lost his job and we were about to lose the house. I did all the cleaning and the cooking until I rebelled and blamed him for my mother's death. What I should have been doing was standing by my dad and helping him. Then I started drinking and arguing just like him. Stealing money out of his wallet when he got drunk just to buy me something to drink. Even sold some of my clothes. I totally went against everything that my mom taught me about You and started following behind my dad's footsteps. When my mom was alive, she would take me to church with her every Sunday. She tried so very hard to get my dad to go but he didn't believe in You like my mom did. Every Sunday morning mom would get my clothes ready first for Sunday school and the for worship service. Yes Lord, my mom had two sets of clothes for me to wear for church. She said the reason for that was that in Sunday school we played games and did a lot of drawing and painting and she wanted me to look nice when it was time for worship service. As for my dad. Well, he just sat in his favorite chair in the living room focused on the TV waiting for a football game to come on. Or any type of sports. He kept making promises that he would go to church with us. But he never did. Except that one time at my mom's funeral. After the funeral that's when he told me that You didn't exist. Because if You did, You wouldn't have taken my mother from him. But, as I found myself falling in that same old black hole as my dad, I started to wonder if You really do exist. And the more I drank, the more I didn't believe in You. Oh Lord, I'm so very tired right now. I'm living from one shelter to another. And my drinking hasn't stopped that much. And when I think of my mom, I would make sure that I find enough to drink so that I would pass out. Please Lord help me. I'm at the end of my rope. Take this life of mine that I may be at peace and away from this world. I hope that You heard me Lord and grant me this one prayer. Please.

My Child;

Most assuredly, I say to you that you will weep and lament, but the world will rejoice; and you will be sorrowful. But your sorrow will be turned into joy. A woman, when she is in labor, has sorrow because her hour has come. But soon as she has given birth to the child, she no longer remembers the anguish. For joy, that a human being has been born into the world. Therefore, you now have sorrow; but I will see you again and your heart will rejoice and your joy no one will take from you. And in that day, you will ask Me nothing. Most assuredly, I say to you, whatsoever you ask the Father in My name I will give you. Until now, you have asked nothing in My name. Ask, and you will receive, that your joy may be full. You have so much to live for in this life. I will not take your life as you have asked of Me. But I will grant you a new life in Me. You are My child. Seek Me; for I am here.

My Lord; My Father; My Deliverer;

Since I was a little girl, I have always called on You in my prayers for my family, my friends, even my enemies for You to bless them. For those who are lost, seeking their way back to You. My prayers were for the homeless and for the children. For the sick and for the bereaved. But, at this moment, right now oh Lord, this time it's personal. I need You more than ever. I have been diagnosed with inoperative breast cancer. My doctors tell me that I have 5 to 6 months left to live. I am so afraid. But I believe in my heart and spirit that my time will come when You say it's my time. My faith, my trust in You couldn't be no stronger than it is now. My fear isn't for myself, but for my husband and my 3 children. They are not aware of my condition. For the past 8 months, I have been going to my doctor and having tests done at the hospital without my husband's knowledge. So far I've been doing pretty good in hiding it. I even went as far as to have a separate life insurance policy made out, so that when my time comes, my husband will have the finances to take care of all the arrangements. You see Lord, breast cancer took my grandmother, my mother and two of my sisters, and my favorite aunt. When my aunt Susan was diagnosed with breast cancer, her husband William and their children were there for her. Her husband showed no weakness and her children were very helpful. I knew that in their hearts they were saddened, but they didn't show it. She went on about her days as if nothing was wrong until it was time for her to leave. And even then, her family stayed by her bedside until her final breath. I don't think my husband will be able to handle it. When my mom and auntie Susan died, my husband took it very hard. It was as if he lost his mother and aunt. He still lives with the loss. Aunt Susan told him before she died to continue being the man, the husband and the father that God created him to be, and that she will always be there for him. So now You can see Lord, on how difficult it would be to tell my husband. As for my children. Oh Lord, my children. I just don't know how to tell them. Stevie, who is 12 years old, dreams of becoming a doctor and scientist in hopes of finding a cure for cancer. Allen, who is 9 years old, wants to be an artist like his dad. And my baby girl, Kathy, who is only 5 years old, wouldn't understand why mommy is gone. My Lord; I just don't know what to do or what to say to my family. It's easy for people to lose faith when pain is plaguing their mind, body and soul. But there is one thing that will never fail to bring peace of mind, and that is my faith. No matter how bad the pain gets, I can count on finding strength in Your word, oh Lord. Your word reminds me that Your healing ministry is pivotal to Your mission, and that even before Your birth, Your Father promised healing to the people of Israel. But yet, it is still hard to except my fate. It's hard, so hard to except the fact that I will not be able to see Stevie become that doctor; Allen become the famous artist. Even see my baby girl walk down the aisle at her wedding. I'm going to miss so much of my children's lives. My husband, my babies, my grandchildren. Oh Lord God; please give me the strength to stand. Give me the courage to tell them. Place the words in my mind and in my heart. Please Father, in the mighty name of Yeshua, my Savior, tell me what to do and strengthen me to do it.

My child;

You are carrying a load that you do not have to carry alone. I am by your side as you go through this part of your life. When I was nailed to the cross and dying, it wasn't death that troubled my heart. It was that I will have to leave behind those that I hold so dear to my heart. But they knew that they will see me again. That is the most difficult and heartbreaking fact that we all must face one day. But I will say this to you My child. You have nothing to fear. For your faith and trust in Me has cleansed you. Be of good cheer; your faith has made you well. Now, go in peace and be a living testimony throughout the land. Return to your own house and tell what great things that My Father has done for you. You are My child, My daughter, in whom I am proud of. Now, go.

Dear God;

What am I to do? When I was 8 years old, I would see my dad hit my mom a lot. She would never fight back. Sometimes he would hit her so hard that it would knock her to the floor. One day when my dad came home from work, my mom had dinner cooked, the house cleaned and all his clothes clean, folded and ironed as if we had a maid living with us. As my dad walked in the house, my mom would greet him at the door with a can of beer and his house shoes in her hands. She would bend down to take off his work boots and put his slippers on his feet and then open his can of beer. His newspaper and the remote control would be on the arm of his favorite chair in the living room. And the TV would be on his favorite channel. He looked very tired and upset as if his was the worse day of his life. I sat on the couch when I heard my mom ask my dad how his day at work was. With an angry look on his face, my dad got out of his chair and walked past me as if I didn't exist and walked into the kitchen for another beer. He didn't say one word. He looked at my mom with a disgusting look on his face. It was a hateful look. Then he walked back to his chair and sat. My mom smiled at me and told me that my dad had a hard day's work and he was very tired. My mom called us to the dinner table. No one was able to sit at the table until my dad sat down first. While my mom was praying, I would take a peek through my fingers and look at my dad. And he looked as if he couldn't wait until my mom finished so he could start and argument. When she was finished praying, she would get out of her chair to go and fix my dad his plate. When she sat back down, she would fix my plate and then hers. But for some reason this day was different. Why? Because on a normal day, my dad would start an argument at the dinner table. On this day, he thanked my mom. He even called my mom sweetheart. Me and my mom looked at each with surprise. I thought to myself, "Wow! We are actually going to have a peaceful family dinner for a change." Then my mom asked my dad how his day at work was. He looked at my mom as if she just destroyed his life and yelled at her, "What the hell you mean how was my day!" He took his plate of food and threw it at my mom and the plate hit her on the head. Then he got up from his chair, threw it to the floor and went into the kitchen and got another can of beer. He walked back to the table, opened up the can, took a big swallow. My dad looked at me. That's when my mom told me to take my dinner to my room because my dad was not feeling well. As I grabbed my plate and headed out of the dining room, my dad turned to my mom and screamed at her, "What in the hell do you mean I'm not feeling well? I turned and looked at my dad. "You think there's something wrong with me you bitch?" Next thing I saw was this can of beer hit my mom in the face. "Go to your room!" my dad shouted at me. I looked at my mom as she grabbed a towel and put on her face because she was bleeding from being hit with the beer can. Then my dad raised his hand at me and shouted again. "Dammit! I said take your ass upstairs to your room you little bitch!" I put my plate back on the dining room table and ran upstairs. But, before I reached the top, I heard a loud crash that stopped me in my tracks. Then there came a moment of silence, a silence that has never been in our house. Running back downstairs and into the kitchen, I saw my dad standing over my mom and he was holding a black iron skillet in his hand. There was blood all on the floor as my mom laid there unconscious. My dad had a fear in his eyes as if he had killed her. He then looked at me, dropped the skillet and ran out the house. I grabbed some towels from the bathroom and ran back to my mom and put the towels on her head to stop the bleeding. As she started to wake up, she looked at me and told me that she was going to be alright. I ran to the living room and called the ambulance, then ran back to my mom. She was sitting in a chair holding the towels to her head. I told her that I called the ambulance and that they are on their way. When the ambulance arrived, the police were with them. They asked my mom what had happened. She told them that she was standing on a chair when she leaned over and fell and hit her head on the countertop. But they knew better. The policeman asked me where my father was. Before I could say a word, my mom told them that he was at work. They put my mom in the ambulance, and I asked if I could go with her. They said it was ok. When we got to the hospital, they rushed my mom to the emergency room. They told me that I had to wait in the waiting room while the doctors worked on my mom. I sat there for about 3 hours when I saw my dad run in asking where my mom was and that he wanted to see her. A doctor walked over to my dad and as they were talking, I snuck in the emergency room to find my mom. When I found the room she was in, she had her head wrapped up and it looked like she was sleeping. So, I sat in a chair next to her and held her hand. That's when my dad walked in. He looked at me with tears in his eyes. He grabbed me and held me in his arms. "Baby, I am so sorry for the things I said to you and your mom. Please forgive me." "I forgive you dad and I still love you," I told him. He then looked at my mom and started crying. He walked up to her bed and laid his head on her chest begging for her to forgive him and that he will never raise his hand to hurt her ever again. And that he will never disrespect her ever again. That's when I saw my mom open up her eyes. She placed her hand on my dad's head and told him that she forgives him. Since that day, my dad has never hit nor cursed at my mom or me ever. He even goes to church with us on Sunday. Now Lord, You may wonder why I am telling You all of this. It's because I am in a relationship that is much like my mom's and dad's relationship before the accident. My boyfriend is physically and emotionally abusive towards me and my son. Things are different these days compared to when my mom and dad were. Jason, who is my boyfriend, makes a lot of money and he has threatened to take my son from me. I don't know what to do or where to go. My mom and dad have passed away and it's just me and my son Eric. Please God help me. Please, in the name of Jesus.

My Child;

Remember the teachings of My servant Peter, when it was said; For to this you were called, because Christ also suffered for us, leaving us an example, that you should follow His steps. Who committed no sin, nor was deceit found in His mouth. Who, when He was reviled did not revile in return. When He suffered, He did not threaten, but committed Himself to Him who judges righteously. Who Himself bore our sins in His own body on the tree, that we, having died to sins, might live for righteousness; by whose stripes you were healed. So, understand My child that My Son has paid the price. You need not get beat nor abused for false love. For My Son is love; real love; true love; pure love. Know My Son and know of His love, then you will know My love for you and your child.

Heavenly Father;

From the time I was 6 years of age, living in Pakistan, my father would take me and my mother to the Mosque to pray. Yes Father, I was raised a

Muslim. At the age of 12 my mother died, and my father continued raising me. He never re-married nor did he have a special woman in his life. I would get up early in the morning, before the sun came up and I and my father would start praying just as soon as we saw the sun rise in the east. We would do this every morning and every night as we saw the sun going down. My father is a devoted Muslim and I wouldn't do anything to disappoint him. And now that I am 16 years of age, my father has planned out my whole life for me. Where I'll be going to school; what I'll be studying; what type of employment I would have. He even went as far as to choose the man I will marry and have children by. One day while I was in the kitchen getting dinner ready, my father came into the house calling out for me. I told him that I was in the kitchen preparing dinner. He ran into the kitchen so fast he almost fell. He had this big smile on his face as if he had won a lot of money. He told me to sit because he had some great news for me. As I sat at the table waiting to hear this great news, my father sat down, pulled an envelope out of his shirt pocket and he asked me if I knew what was in this envelope. I told him no father, what's in it. He ripped it open and read it. Then he looked at and smiles with tears in his eyes. "Daughter, you have been accepted at one of the most highly recommended schools in the United States of America. I asked him what school. He said with a loud and joyous voice, "M.I.T.!" My heart dropped with excitement. As we were celebrating, I asked my father when I am to leave for America. He said as soon as he speaks with the minister at the Mosque, get my physical, get my government and traveling paper and my passport. Basically, in about 3 months. My father has worked so hard to see that I have the education that he never received. So, for the next 3 months my father worked extremely hard and many long hours to get the money that I will need when I leave. He went as far as to go to the bank and took out a loan. He wanted to make sure that I had a need for nothing while living in America. On my final day, for the second time in my life I saw my father cry. He didn't even cry at the death of my mother. It was a quiet drive all the way to the airport. Once there, my father took my bags out of the car and began walking through the terminal as we heard the announcement that the flight to America will be boarding at gate number 6 in 45 minutes. Once at the gate, my father looked at me. "What's wrong father?" I asked him. He looked at me with a smile on his face and said, "You look just like your mother. She would be proud of you if she could see you now." Then my father hugged me and prayed with me. When they called for my flight, my father walked me up to the ticket agent and gave them my ticket. As I started to board, my father yelled out to me "Never forget the things that I have taught you my daughter and give all praise and glory to Allah." It was a long flight. 19 hours. I couldn't wait to get to America. Once there, I called my father to let him know I got there safe. There was a limo there waiting for me when I arrived to take me to the school. Once I got registered for all my classes and got settled in, things were going so well. I kept in touch with my father every day. I still got up just before dawn and said my prayers, studied the Karan and my schoolwork, until I met this young man. His name is Solomon and he is a Christian. He's in a couple of my classes and we study together. One day he asked me for my permission to take me out to lunch. No one has ever asked me for my permission to take me anywhere. I was so enthused, I told him yes. We talked about our lives and our homes. He's from Israel. We got along really well. We even talked about me being a Muslim and him being a Christian. I asked him if he has a problem with that. He said that it's what is in your heart and spirit that God looks at, not what religion you are. Then he told me about Your Son Jesus Christ. I was never told about Him from my father. The only thing my father said is that He was just a prophet like Muhammad. But I learned that He was so much more. Later, as time went on, me and Solomon fell in love. Not just with each other. I fell in love with You and Your Son. But we had one major problem, our families. I love Solomon and he loves me and neither one of our families will agree to us getting married. I love my father, Lord. I would never do anything to disappoint him. And I'm quite sure that Solomon has the same problem as I do. In fact, he has talked to me about how his family and the young Christian girl they have prepared for him to take as his wife. I am caught between a rock and a hard place. Bringing both families together is going to be like an unstoppable force meeting an immovable object. I really need Your help Father. Please tell me what to do and how to do it, in Jesus name, I pray. Amen..

My precious child;

You and Solomon are My servants, My children. Keep your eyes on Me My daughter. For your faith and your trust in Me, as well as your devoted love for My Son truly pleases Me. Remember My servant David when he lifted his voice unto Me and said, "Praise the Lord! Praise, o servants of the Lord! Praise the name of the Lord! Blessed be the name of the Lord from this time forth and forevermore! From the rising of the sun to its going down. The Lord's name is to be praised. The Lord is high above all nations. His glory above the heavens. Who is like the Lord our God; who dwells on high; who humbles Himself to behold the things that are in the heavens and in the earth? He raises the poor out of the dust and lifts the needy out of the ash heap, that He may seat him with princes; with the princes of His people. He grants the barren woman a home, like a joyful mother of children. Praise the Lord!" With that said, My daughter; I am going to leave you and My son Solomon with these words from My others servant Paul. "Speaking to one another in Psalms and hymns and spiritual songs, singing and making melody in your hearts to the Lord, giving thanks always for all things to God the Father in the name of our Lord Jesus Christ, submitting to one another in the fear of God. Wives, submit to your own husband as to the Lord. For the husband is the head of the wife, as also Christ is head of the church; and He is the Savior of the body. Therefore, just as the church is subject to Christ, so let the wives be to their own husband in everything. Husbands, love your wives just as Christ also loved the church and gave Himself for her, that He might sanctify and cleanse her with the washing of water by the word, that He might present her to Himself a glorious church; not having spot or wrinkle or any such thing, but that she should be holy and without blemish. So, husbands ought to love their own wives as their own bodies; he who loves his wife loves himself." So, My daughter, may the marriage between you and Solomon be in truth and in love, first in your Father who is in heaven and to each other. I bless this marriage. I love you My children.

Dear Heavenly Father;

I need You more now than I have ever needed anyone in my life. My life is spiraling downward. I'm at the end of my rope. And I do mean rope.

As I sit here writing You this letter, I have this long rope I found on the streets. And yes Father, the thought of suicide has crossed my mind. But I'm too afraid to do it. I am truly one of Your lost children and I am trying to find my way back to You, but I don't know which way to go, which way to turn. I am the fourth child of six children. My mom, whom I love so much doesn't love me anymore. Sometimes I feel that she never did. I think she only had me so that she can get more money from the government. At times, I wish she would have aborted me to save me the pain that I am going through now. Then my soul and spirit would stay with you forever. I can only remember bits and pieces of my childhood. And the best parts are of those of my granny. I can remember my granny taking care of me when my mom was doing drugs. I can remember my granny taking me to church with her every Sunday in hopes that I would learn more about You. My granny went as far as to obtain full custody of me through the courts. But I rebelled against her in so many ways because I wanted the love from my mother, on which I never received. I remember sitting in my granny's house watching TV when I would hear a car pulling up in her driveway. As I looked out the window to see who it was, I noticed that it was my mother in a different car with a different man inside. As I walked in the kitchen and sat at the table waiting to see her, she would walk in the house and walk right pass me as if I didn't exist. She wouldn't even stop to say hello or nothing. She would walk right upstairs to my granny's room and start arguing with her about how she is raising me. Yelling and cursing at granny as if she was a stranger on the streets. Then it got really quiet. My mother would come storming down the stairs. "Get your damn clothes. You're coming with me for the weekend. Do it now and I don't want to hear a damn word from you," she would say. Why do my mother hate my granny so much Lord? Why? All granny ever tried to do was help my mother. I don't understand it. But that wasn't the worse time of my life. The worse time of my life Lord was when my mother took me to this big city to live with her and her new boyfriend. Once we got to the city, my mother was driving; she pulled the car over to the side of the road, got out of the car, walked over to the side I was sitting on, opened the door and took my bags out the back seat and she took me by the arm and pulled me out the car and threw me to the ground. She looked at me and said, "You are not going to ruin my relationship with my new husband you dirty little bitch. Now find your way back to your damn granny." Then she got back in the car and drove off. As I saw my mother drive off, I was hoping and praying that she would turn around and come back for me. But she didn't. With tears in my eyes and crying out for my mother, she kept going until I couldn't see the car any more. She didn't even look back. There I was; a 12 year old girl, left on the streets in a strange city. Abandoned by my mother, with nowhere to go and knowing no one at all. I just stood there crying as people walked by without saying one word. It was as if Satan ripped my soul right out of me. I prayed to You Father that You would send my mother back for me. As night fall was approaching, I realized that she wasn't coming back for me at all. Reality finally set in and I stopped crying. No child should never have to feel what I felt. That total feeling of loneliness and abandoned. Living on those streets, I did things that I was not proud of. But I had to eat and sleep. One day as I was searching for food in a garbage dumpster, this lady dressed in a business suit and carrying a briefcase, asked me why was I eating out of a dumpster and where were my parents. I told the lady that I was hungry and that both my parents were dead. She asked me if I would like to go get something to eat and take a bath and put on some clean clothes. I asked her, "For what. So you could take me back to my mother?" I told her no. Just then a police officer walked up to the lady and asked her if she needed any help. The lady told the officer that everything was under control. The lady turned around and waved her hand as to signal someone. I got really scared. So, I turned and started to run until I heard someone call out my name. I stopped and turned around to see who was calling me. It was my Uncle Clifford and my granny, standing next to a police car. With tears in my eyes, I ran as fast as I could to her. She grabbed me and hugged me. "Baby I'm so sorry for letting you go with your mother. But it's ok now. I will never let you go again," she said. I asked her if she has seen my mother.

She said that she hasn't heard from her since we left her house. To this day I will never forget how my mother left her 12-year-old daughter on the streets. No matter what my mother has done to me, she is still my mother and I love her no matter what. But now that I am 16 years old and pregnant, not knowing who the father is, I am so afraid that I might turn out like my mother. Please help me Father. Take me back oh Lord. Please.

My Daughter;

Always remember that I love you and whatever you ask in My name, that I will do, that the Father may be glorified in the Son. If you ask anything in My name, I will do it. If you love Me, keep My commandments and I will pray the Father, and He will give you another Helper, that He may abide with you forever; the Spirit of Truth, whom the world cannot receive, because it neither sees Him nor knows Him, for He dwells with you and will be with you. I will not leave you orphan; I will come to you. A little while longer and the world will see Me no more. But you will see Me. Because I live, you will live also. At that day you will know that I am in My Father, and you in Me, and I in you.

Dear Father;

In the mighty name of Jesus, please put my mind and my heart at peace. I don't know where else to turn to. I'm in a very loving relationship with my husband. We worship and adore You with all our mind, heart and spirit. We gather with our brothers and sisters in Christ every Sunday and Wednesday. My husband is not only a good man, but a respectable, responsible and honorable man who fears You. Every night before we go to bed, we give You thanks for all of Your blessings. He is a man who always asking for blessings for me and for others, even his enemies, before he asks for himself. We have been blessed with wonderful jobs, a beautiful home and a strong feeling of security in Your Son Jesus Christ. At the end of every prayer, my husband would always say "The Lord gives and the Lord takes away. Blessed be the name of the Lord." But, when we lie down to sleep, he falls asleep right away as I lie there being haunted by my past; a past that will not let me be. Two months ago, my husband asked, "Let's have a child blessed by God." I was shocked. I asked him if we were ready and able to have a child. He looked at me with astonishment and responded by saying, "Yes we are. Jehovah God has blessed us for our obedience and our faith and trust in Him." So, I agreed that we have a child. He grabbed my hands and we kneeled on the floor as my husband began to pray. "Heavenly Father, the Creator and the Maker of our souls. We ask Your blessings in the name of Jesus as You prepare us to bring a child into this world and into our lives. We seek Your guidance and Your grace that we will raise this child in the way that You desire us to, in spirit and in truth. Thank You LORD Jehovah God in the precious name of Your loving Son, our Lord and Savior Jesus Christ. Amen." And I responded in kind, "Amen." When we stood up, he took me into his arms and hugged me in a way that he had never hugged me before. Then he kissed me and with a joyous smile on his face, he headed down to the basement to his office singing, "Our God is an awesome God." With a heavy heart Father, how do I tell the man that I love so very much; the man that You placed in my life; the man who loves You so dearly, that I cannot have children. Five years before me and my husband met, I went to go see my doctor, Dr. Anders, and told her that I wanted to have a hysterectomy. "Why?" she asked me. "You're just 23 years old. Are you aware of the complications of such a procedure and that you will never be able to have any children?" I told her that I was aware of the complications, but that I still wanted to have it done. She asked if I wanted to talk about it first. You see LORD, my doctor is more than just a doctor; she's a pastor as well. My pastor. When I was 9 years old, my mom died of cancer and I was raised by my alcoholic dad. On Friday nights my dad would invite some of his friends over for poker night. They would spend all night playing card, getting drunk and talk about women in the worse way. One Friday night, it was Friday Night Football. The Redskins vs the Cowboys. So he invited his friends over. Before his friends arrived, my dad would get me ready for bed; say my prayers with me; tucked me under the covers, kiss me on my forehead and wished me a good night. Before he closed my bedroom door, he would turn on my night light. Once the door was closed, I would get out of bed and walk over to my dresser drawer and pull out a picture of my mom and lay it next to my pillow. As I was about to fall asleep, a knock came at my door. I asked, "Is that you dad?" The voice whispered, "No it's your Uncle Roger." I told him to come in. He peeked his head in the door. "Are you asleep? Did I wake you sweetie?" he asked. I told him no. As he walked towards my bed he asked me what was that on my pillow. I told him it was a picture of my mom. Uncle Roger is my mom's brother. He sat on my bed and asked to see the picture. I gave it to him and as he looked at it he said that I looked just like my mom. I asked him where my dad was. He said that he and some of the guys went to the store and that they will be right back. As he was talking to me, I felt his hand under my blanket and rubbing on my leg. I asked him what he was doing. He told me not to worry and that everything is going to be alright. Then he touched my private parts. I asked Uncle Roger to stop. As I tried to scream, he told me that if I did, that my dad wouldn't believe me over him. Then he started kissing on me. I could smell the alcohol on his breath as he slowly pulled my panties down to my knees. I laid there crying. He told me to keep quiet. Then he got on top of me. And Lord, he hurt me. He hurt me so very bad. When he was done, he told me to go into the bathroom and clean myself up and to hurry up about it. All the time while I was in there, all I could do was cry and asked You Lord why this happened to me. When I came out of the bathroom, he had my bed made up and the blood-stained sheets, he put in a plastic bag. He even had a clean night gown for me to put on. He put me back to bed, kissed me on my forehead and wished me a good night's sleep. Then he walked out of my room as if nothing ever happened. But just before he closed the door, he told me that if I told my dad, that my dad wouldn't believe me, and he would hate me. He said that this would be our little secret. I cried myself to sleep that night. And even to this day, my dad still doesn't know, even though Uncle Roger is dead now. So, you see doctor, why I must have this procedure? My doctor responded with tears in her eyes by saying. "Sweetheart, you must talk to someone about this." Well Lord, I had the procedure done. And I'm 30 years old now. And that is why I'm talking to You about this. I don't know how to tell my husband. What words to say and how to say them. I'm so afraid that he may see me in a different way. He wants a child so bad. Please Heavenly Father. I am begging You. I'm pleading with You in the Holy and mighty name of Jesus to help me. Please. I need some answers.

My Loving Child;

I hear your prayers and I feel your pain and sorrow. Because you believe and have faith in My Son, I will prepare you to stand in the midst of your pain and your sorrow. For as my servant Paul once spoke, "We do not wrestle against flesh and blood, but against principalities, against powers, against rulers of the darkness of this age; against spiritual host of wickedness in high places. Therefore, take up the whole armor of God Jehovah that you may be able to withstand in the evil day, and having done all to stand. Stand therefore, having girded your waist with truth; having put on the breastplate of righteousness, and having shod your feet with the preparation of the Gospel of peace. And above all, taking the shield of faith with which, you will be able to quench all the fiery darts of the wicked one. And take the helmet of Salvation and the sword of the Spirit which is the word of God. Praying always with all prayer and supplication in the Spirit, being watchful to this end with all perseverance and supplication for all the saints. So, you stand tall and firm My daughter and I will stand with you. You will never stand alone. I promise you this. Stand.

Our Father; My Father;

You knew the path of life that I would take way before I was even born. And that path led me to You at this time in my life. So, I am calling on You to deliver me please. My mom and dad have been involved with gangs all their lives. That's how they met. They were rival gang members. But for some strange reason, they got together. I guess it was to keep the peace between the two gangs; the East Side Cobras and the Latin Kings. My mom was the sister of the leader of the Cobras and my dad ran the Latin Kings. I remember how my dad would walk in the house with two or more gunshot wounds and my mom would gather me and my brother up to rush my dad to the hospital. We were at the hospital so much that the police stopped asking questions about what happened, and the doctors knew my dad by his first name. He was like a regular patient. His wounds were never serious. I guess he was just lucky. We lived in a neighborhood where drug and gang violence were as common as regular people getting up early in the morning just to go to work. When I was 12 years old, my mom would go to work for the Cobras, and sometimes she would take me and my little brother, who was 5 years old at the time. Being with her I've seen things that no child should ever have to see; from people using drugs; the selling of drugs and guns; the torture and the beating of either a rival gang member to one of their own; even people having sex in the middle of the floor or in a corner of a room. Me and my brother never went to school. My mom tried to get us in school across town, but my dad told her that me and my brother needed to learn how to survive on the streets if we were to remain alive after they're dead and gone. At age 15, I was running drugs for my dad and sitting in meetings with high level gang member with my mom. As they talked about who should live and who should die; even when it came down to killing children and babies. And my dad would take me on a late-night drive by. One night I was with my dad and he was looking for this dude named Pookie. He said that Pookie stole some money and drugs from him. When my dad saw him walking near Grant Park, he pulled his car to the side of the road. He saw my dad's car as my dad called him over. I guess Pookie thought that my dad forgot about what he did. He walked up to my dad's car and my dad had his gun on his lap. He asked Pookie if he had his money. Just as Pookie was about to go into his pocket, my dad shot him in the head. Then my dad drove off.

I wasn't even scared. That was the first time I saw my dad commit cold blooded murder up close and personal. From that point on, I was not only becoming a product of my environment, but I was also becoming more and more like my mom and dad; the smooth-talking financial wiz like my mom and the cold-blooded killer like my dad. One night as we were all in the living room watching T.V., there came a knock at the back door. My mom told me and my brother to go to our rooms. I ran upstairs quickly to my room and closed my door and hid in a cubby hole in my closet. I thought my little brother was behind me, but he wasn't. Then I heard gun fire, a lot of it. As I sat in that cubby hole, I could hear my mom screaming out for my dad and my little brother's name. Then there were four loud bangs. Then there was silence; as if death walked through our house as a house guest. Too afraid to move, I sat there in that cubby hole, fearing the worse. I stayed in that hole for hours, until I heard voices coming up the stairs. It sounded like the police because I could hear their radios. My dad left a 9mm in the cubby hole and told me one day that if there was any kind of trouble, to take my little brother in there and to shoot anyone who ever tried to get in. I grabbed the gun and pointed it at the door of the cubby hole. That's when someone was trying to open the door. Slowly, a policewoman opened the door and saw a 9mm pointing right in her face. "It's ok sweetie. You can put the gun down. Come on. Hand me the gun," she said. She slowly reached up and took the gun out of my hand. I sat there in that hole as if I was sitting in a 12-foot grave and as I tried to crawl out, the opening seemed to be further and further away. The sun that was shining in that grave got smaller and smaller. As the policewoman walked me down the stairs, I saw my mom and dad lying on the floor dead. My mom had a gunshot wound in her back and one in the back of her head. My dad was on the living room floor with two gunshots to his face. As we walked out the front door, I could see the paramedics working on my little brother. "Wait!" I shouted. As I heard one paramedic say, "We lost the little guy. Call it at 10:46 pm. He didn't have a chance." "I want to see my brother and I want to see him now," I told the officer. Before they took him away, they opened up the bag and I saw my little brother with two bullet holes in his chest. The policewoman asked me if I had any other family to go to. I told her that my mom, my dad and my little brother were my only family. They took me to the police station where I sat in this room for at least 2 hours before this lady in a suit came in and told me that she was going to take me to this place where children have nowhere to live. This place was filled with a lot of kids my age; boys and girls. I stayed there until I was 17 years old before I ran away. I found myself living on the streets. Living the street life as my mom and dad did. I got arrested at the age of 21 for carrying a 9mm and they found 25 bricks of cocaine in the abandon building I was living in. And yes, that cocaine was mine. They also found an AK-47, 100 small baggies of crystal meth, 5 pounds of weed and $30,000.00 in cash. That was mine also. But on my court day, luck would play its part. The woman who represented me was the same policewoman who was there when my family was murdered. She told the judge my story and asked him to have mercy on me due to the circumstances of my life as a child. The judge handed down a 12-year sentence. I was shipped off to a woman's correctional facility in the middle of nowhere. And while being there, I have done really awful things. I've stole, beat up other women, sold drugs, even used Your name in vain. I even have a woman who comes to my cell at night so that I could fulfill my sexual desires. When she would come back at night and sometimes during the day, I would put my celly out so that I can get my row out and have some fun. Now, my celly was in for first degree murder for shooting her boyfriend for beating her half to death, cutting up her face and leaving her to die. She said that when the police found her; she was lying outside on the front lawn, naked and covered in blood. She said she spent 3 weeks in the hospital with 3 broken ribs, a broken arm, and 72 stitches from her belly up to her face. Once she got better and able to walk, she went searching for him. But the thing about that was when she found him. She saw him getting out of his car one day at the local grocery store with another woman hanging on his arm. She said that she walked up to him and shot him once in the leg, once in the growing, once in the belly and twice in the face. Talk about your over-kill. It sounded like she just lost it. She said that her hate came out not so much that he did what he did, but that the judge only gave him 6 months in jail and 6 months' probation. Every night my celly would pray to You to forgive her for taking his life. After she had finished praying, I asked her if You would forgive me for the things I had done. The only thing she told me was, "For God so loved the world that He gave His only begotten Son, that whosoever believes in Him shall not perish, but have everlasting life." Then she went right to sleep. I have so much hate built up in me Father. I need to hear from You Lord. Please make me over. I am sorry for all the hurt and sorrow that I brought in the lives of many people. For once in my miserable life, I am asking for Your help and that Your Son Jesus Christ would come into my life and clean this retched soul of a woman. Please Father, in the name of Jesus.

My Child;

You have called upon Me and I hear your prayer. And I will answer it. My son David called on Me as you have. And this is what he said. "Have mercy upon me oh God; according to Your loving-kindness; according to the multitude of Your tender-mercies. Blot out my transgressions; wash me thoroughly from my iniquity and cleanse me from my sins. For I acknowledge my transgressions and my sins is always before me. Against You, You only, have I sinned and done this evil in Your sight. That You may be found just when You speak and blameless when You judge. Behold, I was brought forth in iniquity and in sin my mother conceived me. Behold, You desire truth in the inward parts and in the hidden part You will make me to know wisdom. Purge me with hyssop, and I shall be clean. Wash me, and I shall be whiter than snow. Make me hear joy and gladness; that the bones You have broken may rejoice. Hide Your face from my sins and blot out all my iniquities. Create in me a clean heart, O God, and renew a steadfast spirit within me. Do not cast me away from Your presence, and do not take Your Holy Spirit from me. Restore to me the joy of Your salvation and uphold me by Your generous Spirit. Then I will teach transgressors Your ways, and sinners shall be converted to You. Deliver me from the guilt of bloodshed, O God; the God of my salvation, and my tongue shall sing aloud of Your righteousness. O Lord, open my lips and my mouth shall show forth Your praise. For, You do not desire sacrifice, or else I would give it. You do not delight in burnt offerings. The sacrifices of God are a broken spirit; a broken and contrite heart. These, O God, You will not despise. Do good in Your good pleasure to Zion. Build the walls of Jerusalem; then You shall be pleased with the sacrifices of righteousness, with burnt offerings and whole burnt offerings. Then they shall offer bulls on Your alter." So, you see my daughter. David's prayer of redemption was sincere just as yours is sincere and from your heart, which I look at. Though David's sacrifice was burnt offerings, My Son was the sacrifice for you. Know of His love for you and except His love which is from Me, your Father. Let Him enter your life that your spirit may be set free.

Dear Jehovah God;

I have been a devoted Christian all my life. But, living here in Somalia is so very hard for a Christian; even harder for a Christian woman. I know that one day You will deliver me from the pain and the suffering that I am enduring. I have 9 children and 4 of my children were born due to being raped and I'm only 28 years old. My husband was killed by the rebels because he would not join their cause, but mostly because he too was a Christian. After his death, me and my oldest son were going to take the children and run to the nearest Christian mission we could find, which was about 15 miles away. But we didn't make it. We tried to leave at night, in hopes that we wouldn't be seen. That's when the rebels came. They killed all the infants and the elders and they took all the children. Children that were old enough to carry a gun. They were about to take my children until I pleaded with them. But they took my eldest son. Then they raped and beat me right in front of my other children. After they were done, they left, taking my son with them. I will continue to fight to find my son. We walked for miles trying to find help. During that time, I buried 3 of my children to sickness. And now, I am pregnant again. We reached Mogadishu when my water broke. And right there in the middle of the street, I gave birth to a beautiful baby girl. An old woman dressed as a Muslim came to my aid. "God bless you and Jesus keep you," I told her. She looked at me. "You're a Christian, aren't you?" she asked. "Yes, I am," I said to her, with fear in my eyes that she might turn me over to the rebels and take my children away from me. She said to me "All Muslims are not rebels. There are those who believe in love and peace with all mankind. Come with me my child and let's get these children off the streets and get you some medical attention especially for your newborn." She took off her head dress and wrapped my baby in it as we proceeded to walk away from all the violence that was going on in the city. As we were walking, a truck full of rebel soldiers were headed our way. She grabbed my hand and rushed me and my children into a building that was filled with women and children. They were hiding from either being killed, raped or their children taken away. I asked the old woman, "Are all these women Christian?" She said, "No, they're Muslim. The rebels don't care if you're Christian or Muslim. They just enjoy raping women and children. I sat helpless as the rebels raided our village and killed my husband and my sons, and brutally raped my daughter and her two little girls, and then they shot all three of them in the head and cut off their heads when they were done. Then they took their bodies and burned them and place their heads on sticks and stuck them in the ground right in the middle of our village." I was totally surprised to hear such a story by a Muslim. The old woman told us to have a seat and to stay quiet, she'll be right back. I was so afraid that she would bring back the rebels because she was gone for a long time. So me and my children got up and headed towards the back exit of the building. "Wait!" the old woman yelled. "Where are you going and where are you taking those children." When I turned around, the old woman was carrying three baskets of food and with her was this white lady, who was a doctor. "I told you that if you leave the rebels will surly kill you and your children," the old woman said. I told her that I was afraid for the lives of my children. Then the old woman took my hand and said, "If you don't trust me, then trust God. I am not here to hurt you nor cause hurt to come to your children. Now sit and let the doctor look at you and your children." While the doctor was seeing to my children, the old woman asked me why was I here in the city where there's nothing but death all around us. I told her that I am looking for my eldest son who was taken by the rebels. "Just stay here with us for a while until you're strong enough to leave on your own. Then if you want to leave then you can, okay?" she said. So, me and my children stayed there. That night while my children were asleep, the old woman came and woke everyone up. "Get up everyone! Get up now!" the old woman screamed. "What's going on?" I asked. She told us that the leader of the rebels, Mohammed Siad Barre just arrived in the city and he's killing any and all women and children. In my heart, all that I could feel was, "Father in Heaven, how much longer will You allow this to go on; how long oh Lord." As we gathered our children and headed out the back of the building, we could hear the horrifying screams of women being tortured and shot. Then the screams of children as they were being killed. The sounds of crying babies and then their silence followed by a gunshot. We quietly and very cautiously made our way through the city.

On our way, I have never in my life seen so many piles upon piles of children's bodies torn apart by these men. Father, how can men do such hideous and ungodly things to children. How, oh Lord. Please tell me how. When we reached the end of the city, the rebels had a display of men and women hanging on crosses with their bodies riddled with bullets. All 30 of us women, including the white doctor, cried and prayed. The last cross we saw was that of a pregnant woman whose baby was cut out of her body and the baby lay at the foot of that cross, still with the umbilical cord attached. The white doctor walked over to see about the baby. She looked at the old woman and shook her head as to say that the baby was dead. We walked until daylight, when we saw an U.N. truck convoy.

They stopped and put us all on the truck and turned around and headed for the safety zone. Once in the safety zone, me and my children were able to get the help that we needed. I looked around to find the old woman, but she was nowhere to be found. It was as if she just disappeared. I had a picture of my eldest son, walking around asking if anyone has ever seen him. No one seemed to know who he was. Then I walked upon this man who was a Muslim. I showed him the picture and asked if he has seen my son. He said that he hasn't seen such a boy in the camp. But he will look for him if I wish it so. He took the picture. I asked him to please bring it back to me, for that was the only picture I had of him. He said that he would bring it right back. Me and my children went into our tent to rest. Hours had gone by with no word from the man, until he walked into our tent and told me that he searched all over the camp, but didn't see my son. I started to cry. The man told me that Allah will unite me and my son together; on earth or in heaven. And then he started praying for me. I didn't understand his language, but I knew that he was praying. We stayed there in the camp for at least 17 months and that man saw to it that me and my children had all that we needed. He told me that he works for an organization in the United States called "Find The Children." As time went on, me and the man, whose name is Absalom, got married. 8 months later, I found myself living in Nigeria and pregnant, about to give birth to twin boys. I will never forget about my son. And no matter where he is, I know that You are watching over him Father. By the way LORD, Absalom converted over to Christianity. One evening while the children was in their rooms and I was preparing dinner, I heard my husband coming through the door. "I'm home," he shouted. "Come help me," he said. I took off my apron and walked through the house, to the front door. I could see that he had some luggage in his hand. He said that there was more in the car. I asked him who this luggage belongs to. As my husband came in the house, a young man walked in right behind him. I was speechless. It was my son. All that I could do was cry tears of joy. I grabbed him and hugged him. And coming right behind my son was the old woman who got me and my children out of Mogadishu. Father in heaven, You have answered all my prayers. It was a most joyous occasion. But, at times I still have nightmares of those days back in Somalia, and the children that I buried there. It still haunts me. But I know Father that You will one day unite all of us together again. One day Father. One day.

My Daughter; My Child;

Listen closely to the story in which I am about to tell you and place these words within your heart and spirit. Know that when you were in trouble, I was there. When you feared for the loss of your husband and your children, I was there. So listen and know that I am always there for you and will never leave you nor abandon you. You are My child. "A certain man went down from Jerusalem to Jericho and fell among thieves who stripped him of his clothing, wounded him and departed, leaving him half dead. Now, by chance a certain priest came down that road. And when he saw him, he passed by on the other side. Likewise, a Levite, when he arrived at the same place, came and looked, and passed on the other side. But a certain Samaritan, as he journeyed, came where he was and when he saw him, he had compassion. So, he went to him and bandaged his wounds, pouring on oil and wine; and he set him on his animal, brought him to an inn, and took care of him. On the next day, when he departed, he took out two denarii, gave them to the innkeeper and said to him, "Take care of him and whatever more you spend, when I come again, I will repay you." So, tell Me, My child. Which of these three do you think was neighbor to him who fell among the thieves? And know this daughter of Mine; that your sorrow is only for a time. And God will wipe away every tear from your eyes; there shall be no more death, nor sorrow, nor crying. There shall be no more pain; for the former things have passed away. I am with you My child, My daughter.

Dear Lord;

I am so lost and no one to turn too. No one to confine in but You. I need You Lord. I need for You to help me find a solution to this desperate situation. I'm 20 years old now and at one time I was pregnant, and the father was my ex-boyfriend, who raped me. I was very frightened of him because he would beat me if things didn't go his way. But I loved him. I always wondered who my mom and dad were, and if my dad treated my mother that way. I lived with my grandmother all my life. I spent many years searching for my mom, but with no success. I used to ask grandmother about my mom, but she wouldn't want to talk about her. She always walked away from the conversation. And when I would reach out to other family members, they would look at me as if I did something wrong, something truly evil. It was as if they hated me for reason that I did not know of. As I was sitting in my bedroom, my grandmother knocked on the door. I told her to come on in. When she walked in, she pulled up a chair in front of me and looked me straight in my eyes. I asked her what was going on. "I need to talk to you about your mother," she said. I quickly stopped doing what I was doing and turned off my computer. She took a deep breath. "I need you to listen and not say one word until I am done. Your mother was a very loving woman. You look so much like her that the two of you could be sisters. She was very well loved in our neighborhood. She was always helping people at the shelter and always doing her part at the church functions. She was a very quiet and peaceful woman, but most importantly, she loved the Lord. She had a job at the local hardware store as a cashier. Sometimes Mr. Henry would let her close up at night so that she can make a little more money. One night, as she was closing up, a man rushed in as she was walking out and told her to lock the door. He forced her to the back of the store and raped and beat your mother half to death. He never took any money or merchandise. Your mother was able to crawl to the phone in the store to call the police. When they got there, she was laying on the floor bloodied and naked, fighting for her life." While my grandmother was telling me this, tears came running down my face and my heart was torn apart. "When they got her to the hospital, they rushed her straight to the operation room. That man cut your mother's throat and cut up her body like she was a piece of meat. Me and your grandfather stayed in her room with her for five weeks. Many nights, she would have nightmares. But we stayed by her side. The doctors were not sure if she would ever wake up again. They said that the traumatic event that happened to her is still set in her sub-conscience mind. That is why she is reacting the way she is. No one else in the family came to see your mother. Your grandfather would leave the hospital to go check on the house and bring me a change of clothes every day that I was there. One day, a police detective came to the room. He asked if he could speak to your grandfather alone. Your grandfather told him that whatever he has to say, that he could say it right there with the both of us. The detective told us that they didn't find any fingerprints and they didn't have anything to go on to find the man that did this. But they are working on it. In other words, the man got away. After the detective left, we heard a moan coming from your mother. She had awakened. One week later we were able to take her home. There were many nights that your mother woke up soaked in sweat. It took a long time for her to leave the house, let alone the bedroom. Three months after that, she found out that she was pregnant. That's when her whole world came crashing down around her. On the day her water broke, and she was going into labor, I took her to the hospital. I stayed in the delivery room with her. And when you were born, the nurse wrapped you up and handed you to your mother and your mother turned away in tears. She asked the nurse that she needed to speak to someone from the Department of Children and Family Services or an Adoption Agency. I looked at her and asked her is that what she really wanted to do. She said it was exactly what she wanted and needed to do for the sake of the baby. Me and your grandfather wanted to adapt you, but the state said that we were a little too old to care for and infant; that the baby would be better off with a young family. The day we left the hospital, your mother had no words to say about what she had done, nor did she want to talk about it." I asked my grandmother if she knew where my mother was. She told me to let it go. With tears in my eyes, I begged and pleaded with her to tell me where my mother was. She told me to put on some clothes and meet her outside so that she could take me to see my mother. Grandmother was in her car waiting for me. When I got in, she asked me if I was ready for this. I told her that I couldn't be no more ready than what I am now.

My heart was pounding really fast. We drove for a long time, until she started to slow down. She pulled into a cemetery. I asked her why she didn't tell me that my mother was dead. She said that it was better that I know what happened first. "Grandmother, how did she die," I asked. "She died of a broken heart and a broken spirit," she said. When she pulled up to the grave site, I got out of the car and walk up to the tomb stone. It read: Sue Ling; Born: December 25, 1982 – Died: October 5, 2015; Rest in Peace. I stood there for a few minutes. "Hi. I'm your daughter. The one you gave away. The one you never loved. The one you hated. I wasted many years of my life being angry with you and asking why you threw me away like a piece of trash. But I must live with the same pain that you lived with. Because when I was pregnant, I went and had an abortion. I still feel that pain; that loss; empty inside. But I forgive you mother. And I pray that you accepted Christ in your life before you died. I love you mother and goodbye." Then I walked away. That was the last time I spoke to my mother Heavenly Father. My mother gave away her rape baby. But I killed my rape baby. Oh, Heavenly Father, could You ever forgive me for what I have done? How can I redeem myself? How can You ever forgive me when I can't forgive myself?

My Child;

Remember Judas, whom I called friend, betrayed Me with a kiss. Yet, I still loved him. Peter, My most trusted, denied

Me three times. Yet, I still loved him. My own people who condemned Me to death. Yet, I still loved them. The soldiers who beat Me within an inch of My life and cursed and mocked Me. Yet, I still loved them. But the worse pain that I have ever felt in My life was the pain when I took the sins of all mankind upon Myself and at that moment before dying, My Father turned away from Me. That pain of rejection from My Father was worse than any beating that I had received from man. Though He turned away for just a moment, was the hardest thing to face. I cried out to Him and asked, "Why did You forsake Me?" Believe Me child when I tell you that I cried out. And My Father cried for Me. But I now sit on His right side. He never left Me. He was always there. So, My child, know that I will never leave you nor forsake you. By My stripes, My pain, My suffering, the shedding of My blood and your faith in Me and My Father, you are healed. You are forgiven, now go and forgive yourself.

Dear Lord God;

In my country, we as women and mothers stayed at home raising our children and took care of the families. While our husbands worked and provided for the household. My husband is a very successful businessman working for the Indian Oil Company. One day he was given the opportunity to start up another branch of the oil company in another country, which meant that we would have to move away from our home and start a new life somewhere else. It took up to 3 months to get prepared for the journey. Once we reached our destination, we were greeted at the airport by a gentleman driving a stretch limousine. He drove us to this lavish hotel where we would be waited on hand and foot. It was really nice, though I miss my home and my country. But on our way there, I noticed all the poor and starving people on the streets. I thought to myself, "I am so glad that we won't ever have to live like those people." But I also felt so saddened for the children I saw living and eating out of garbage cans. When we reached the hotel, the driver got out and opened the door for us as another man came running out the hotel to get our luggage. As we were following my husband into the hotel, I saw a little boy begging for food. I had a small bag of airline food with me. As I turned to give it to the little boy, my husband ran up to me and told me to not feed the natives because once you do, they will never stop begging or bothering you. I always listened to my husband. My 10-year-old son followed behind his father as my 5 year old daughter followed behind me. My daughter looked at me with the saddest looking eyes and asked me why can't we feed the little boy? "I told her that her father told me not to," I replied. For the next 3 months, we didn't leave that hotel room. If we needed anything the hotel employees would see that we have all that we wanted. One afternoon, while my husband was out, I stood out on the balcony and admired the beauty of the ocean to my right. However, to my left, I would say, at least 100 feet away; there was a small colony of poor women and children digging through the dumpsters looking for food. My heart was filled with sorrow and I felt that I had to do something. So, I changed my clothes to go down there. I was forbidden to remove my head-dress, but I did it anyway. I then went into the kitchen and opened the refrigerator and took some food out and put in in a bag. Just at that moment, my children walked in. "Mother! What are you doing? You took off your head-dress.

Where are you going?" my son asked. "I'll be right back." "But father told us not to leave the hotel," he said. I walked over to my son and kneeled down in front of him and said, "This will be our little secret. There are children eating out of garbage cans and I'm just taking them a little food, that's all," I told him. Frightened, he told me to please hurry back before father gets home. As I walked out the door, I told my son to lock it behind me. I was hoping that the hotel receptionist didn't recognize me without my head-dress. As I was walking past him, he asked if I needed him to call me a taxi. Still walking, I told him that I would be fine, but no thank you. Once outside, I started walking towards where I saw the children. I looked up and I could see my son looking down at me and waving. I didn't wave back because I didn't want anyone to know that I was coming from the hotel. So, I just kept walking towards the children. When I reached to where I saw the children, there were only four or five of them standing there and watching me. I walked up to them and pulled some of the food out of the bag. Before I knew it, I was surrounded by at least 20 more children with their hands out asking for food. I handed out all the food that was in the bag. They all took their food and sat down right in front of me and started eating. I watched as these little babies were eating as if it was their only meal for days, and it probably was. I rushed back into the hotel and to the room; changed my clothes and got dinner on because my husband would be home soon. When dinner was done and the table set, husband walked through the door. I went to greet him, and he looked very tired. So, I took his briefcase and sat it down in the living room. I then took off his suit jacket and laid it on the couch. I told him that dinner was ready and that his bath water was ready. He went into the bathroom to take his bath. When he came out, he asked me if I left the hotel. I told him no. That was the first time that I ever lied to my husband. As the family sat down at the table to eat, my husband told me that the hotel receptionist thought he saw a woman that looked like me leave out this afternoon. "Please forgive me my husband for lying to you. I did go out just for a few minutes. There were these children that were eating out of the garbage, and I had to give them some food." "I specifically told you not to leave the hotel. But most important, I told you not to feed these people. You disobeyed me," he said angrily. "You even took off your head-dress on top of being disobedient," he shouted. He got up from the dinner table and went into our bedroom and slammed the door. I told my children to finish their dinner while I try to talk to their father. I walked to the door and tried to open it, but it was locked. As I was trying to explain to him why I did it, he came rushing out of the room and stormed out the door without saying one word. Later that night after dinner and the children were in bed, I lay in my bed hoping and praying that my husband would come home. I didn't sleep at all for a while, until the door opened and I got out of bed and it was my husband. "Its 2:00 am my husband. Where have you been," I asked him. He didn't say one word. He just went to our room and took a pillow and a blanket off the bed and slept on the couch that night. So, I went back to bed. The following morning, I was awakened by a knock on the front door. As I was putting on robe, they knocked again. I'm coming," I called out. As I walked to the door, I noticed that my husband was no longer here. Maybe he left early for work. When I opened the door, it was the hotel manager. I asked him if there was anything I can do for him. He told me that we would have to vacate the room my 9:00 am. "What!" I said angrily. Then he walked away. My son ran up to me and asked me what was wrong. I looked around the hotel room and all of my husband's clothes were gone. Our passports and any money we had were gone too. My husband left us. I sat on the couch trying to figure out what did I do that was so terribly wrong for my husband, the man I loved, whom I bore his children, to leave us in a strange country with no money and no passport to get back to our home. My son came over and sat next to me crying. I asked him why he was crying. He said that before his father went to take his bath last night, he came and asked me did I leave the hotel, and he said I did. My son told me that he was sorry and that I taught him to never tell a lie. I hugged my son, and my daughter came and sat next to us and I hugged them both and told them that everything was going to be alright. I told my son that he did the right thing and that I am proud of him for being truthful. We gathered all of our things and left the hotel. Not knowing where we were going. Not knowing a soul in a foreign country. As we were walking, my daughter pulled on my dress. As I looked down at her saddened eyes, she told me that she was hungry. My son said that he was hungry as well. We didn't have much food, but I gave it to my children. It was about to get dark and I became frightened for the safety of my children. That's when I saw a large group of children and about 6 adults walking towards us. I picked up my daughter and held her close and pulled my son to me even closer. When the group of children reached us, a little boy, about my son's age, stretched out his hand and gave my daughter a piece of cooked chicken and my son a loaf of bread. Then all of the children encamped around us, along with the 6 adults. They were praying for us in their native tongue. One of the adult women took me by the hand and guided me and my children to a dump site where all of the homeless people lived and put us in this make-shift room. Before she left, she gave us three bottles of water; then she left. Father in heaven, please strengthen my heart and spirit. Thank you for watching over me and my children. If this is where You want us to be, then so be it. Let Your will be done and not mine, oh Lord. And with all that is in my soul, please forgive my husband, as I forgive him.

My Loving Daughter;

So why do you worry about clothing? Consider the lilies of the field, how they grow; neither toil nor spin; and yet I say to you that even Solomon in all his glory was not arrayed like one of these. Now, if God, your Father, so clothed the grass of the field, which today is, and tomorrow is thrown into the oven, will He not much more clothe you? Therefore, do not worry saying, "What shall we eat or what shall we drink." Or "What shall we wear." For after all these things the Gentile seek. For your heavenly Father knows that you need all these things. But seek first the Kingdom of God and His righteousness and all these things shall be added to you. Therefore, do not worry about tomorrow; for tomorrow will worry about its own things. Enough for the day is its own trouble. You have nothing to worry about, my daughter. I have been with you and your children throughout this whole situation, and My Holy Spirit will comfort you and give you peace.

Dear Lord Jesus;

You have blessed me throughout my years. A successful businesswoman; a loving husband who loves You and worships You. A new home and two brand new cars. My husband was even able to start up his own art and photography studio. But with all of this success, comes strong discipline, which I have lost. I was so caught up with the glamour and the worldly things that I totally forgotten who blessed us with all that we have. It started with me bringing in the wrong clients. I hooked up with this big-time movie producer, who was also a big-time drug dealer. I found myself not only using drugs but sleeping with the producer/drug dealer just to keep the account. An account that brought in an additional $15,000.00 a month. I would sometimes go to the bank and withdraw out large amounts of cash and bring it home to my husband as if I had just got paid from this client. One day the producer called me on my cell phone and told me that he has a group of very important businessmen coming over to his place for a dinner party and that he would like for me to be there. It would be my chance to snag the big accounts. He said that each gentleman could net me a possible total of $500,000.00 each. I told him to give me about an hour to get ready and that I will be there. Then he hung up the phone. As I was getting ready, my husband walked in from work. "Honey, I'm home," he shouted. "I'm in the bedroom," I replied. When he walked in the room, he had this smile, this glow as if he had won the lottery. "I just pulled my first big client," he said. Then he reached into his shirt pocket and pulled out a check for $27,000.00. I told him that I was proud of him, but that I have to go to this dinner party that could net me $500,000.00 per person. "I made plans for us to go out tonight and celebrate. I called you and told you this just as soon as my client left my studio. Did you forget?" he said. I told him that I was truly sorry. With a disappointed look on his face he told me to go on ahead to my business meeting. And he wished me good luck, which he has never done. He would always wish me good blessings. Then he left the room and went down stairs. Once I got all my papers in my briefcase, I rushed down the stairs and headed out the door, when I heard him say, "I'll see you tonight." I walked over to him and gave him a peck on his forehead and rushed out the door. When I got in my car, I thought to myself, "I was wrong for treating my husband that way. But, I'm sure he'll understand." I

didn't get home until 4:30 in the morning. When I walked in the house, he was still sitting on the couch, watching T.V. He asked me how the meeting was. I told him that it went very well. And that all I wanted to do was go to bed and sleep. He asked me to come and sit next to him. When I sat down next him, I put my head on his shoulder and sighed as if I was very tired, which I was. Then he asked me about the $5,000.00 that was withdrawn from our account. I told him that I took it out for the meeting I had to go to, but I lied. It was for the drugs that I owed the dealer. Then he held up four small blue baggies and asked me where they came from. I got very upset with him and told him I didn't know where they came from and what was he accusing me of. "I'm not accusing you of anything. I just asked you a question," he responded. "Are you doing drugs?" he asked me. I jump up off the couch and shouted, "Hell No!" Then I headed out the door and into my car. I thought he would at least call me back in the house, or even come after me, but he didn't. So I drove off. I drove to this park about four blocks away from our home and just sat there. Then my cell phone rang. I looked at it and it was my husband. I didn't bother to answer it. He called several times. The last call he made to me, he left a message. This was the message he left me Lord. "Sweetheart, I know that something is wrong. And you know that you can always talk to me. I have never judged you in no form or fashion. We have worked so hard together in our lives that we should be able to trust each other with anything. So whatever that is troubling your heart and spirit, I know that with the help of God and our Lord Jesus Christ, we can get through it together. When you are ready to talk, I'll be here. I am going nowhere and nowhere is going with me. Just come home please. I love you." Oh Lord Jesus. how do I tell my husband that I have a drug problem and that I cheated on him and our marriage? I broke the promise I made to You and to him. I don't want to lose him. No man has ever loved me in my life like my husband. No man has never understood me like my husband. If I tell him, he may walk out of my life forever. That is one thing that I don't think I can handle. Please Lord Jesus, tell me what to do.
Please.

My Child; My Daughter;

Understand that you must be truthful with your husband. No matter what the outcome. You made a promise to Me and to your husband on your wedding day. Hold to your promise.

Do not lay up for yourself treasures on earth, where moth and rust destroy and where thieves break in and steal. But, lay up for yourself treasures in heaven, where neither moth or rust destroys and where thieves do not break in and steal. For where your treasure is, there your heart will be also. The lamp of the body is the eye. If therefore the eye is good, your whole body will be full of light. But, if your eye is bad, your whole body will be full of darkness. If therefore the light that is in you is darkness, how great is that darkness. No one can serve two masters. For either he will hate the one and love the other, or else he will be loyal to the one and despise the other. You cannot serve God and mammon. You say that you trust Me and have faith in me, then show it. Don't just talk about it. You have done wrong to Me, to yourself and to your husband. Go to him and talk to him. I sent him into your life for a reason. Follow the teachings of my servant Paul. "For we walk by faith and not by sight." Now go to your husband with the faith that everything is going to be alright. The healing process will not be easy. But I am with you every step of the way. Now go in peace.

I am a vessel created by the loving hands of God Himself. I am as precious as the many treasures of the Pharaohs; as beautiful as the Queen of Sheba. I am a vessel designed by the mighty hands of God. I am to be filled only with the waters of love and compassion; as if the waters were drawn from the bosom of the Nile herself. I am as gentle as the soft blowing winds of Israel. My spirit shines as bright as the many stars of Lebanon at night; and my heart is as passionate as the petals of the Rose of Sharon; as free as the lilies of the valley. I am a vessel created by the loving hands of God. I am God's vessel. I am woman.

By: S.G.A.

Teach me O Lord, the way of Your statutes, and I shall observe it to the end. Give me understanding, that I may observe Your law and keep it with all my heart. Make me walk in the path of Your commandments, for I delight in it. Psalm 119:33-35

O Lord my God, in You I have taken refuge; Save me from all those who pursue me and deliver me. Or he will tear my soul like a lion; dragging me away, while there is none to deliver.
Psalm 7: 1-2

Heal me, O Lord, and I will be healed. Save me and I will be saved; For You are my praise. Psalm 17:14

A MAN'S CRY FOR HIS FATHER

"A Man's Cry for His Father" are the heart-felt prayers of men who are desperately and honestly seeking their heavenly Father. Whatever their troubles may be, they are calling on God and their Savior for answers. Within each prayer you will find various scriptures from the book of Psalm. When we pray to our Father and our Savior, we tend to think the They will answer us strictly through scripture. But we must understand and acknowledge that They have feelings and emotions. This is why we have feelings and emotions of our own, because they were given to us by our Father when He created us. JAH is not a Father without feelings nor emotions. When His Son died, He cried. He hurts as we hurt. However, His feelings are Holy. His emotions are Holy. And when He answers the prayers of these men, He answers them as a true Father would; with heart and compassion; with understanding and truth; with firmness and with patience; but most importantly with love. A love that cannot compare to that of any earthly father. "A Man's Cry for His Father" shows us how to re-connect that lost Father and son relationship that we so desire to regain with our Heavenly Father and our Lord and Savior. I hope that you will enjoy reading their prayers and that you will share this book with other men, young and old alike. May our Father and our Savior continue to bless you all……..

This book is dedicated to the loving memory of (Allen Henry Wade; Willie T. Gillespie; John Alfred Freeman (Cannon); Jerry Antonio Farrington (Crush). This book is also dedicated to my brothers; Jon Leander Samuels, Ray Anthony Samuels and Christopher Anderson. My nephews, Trevor, Eddie and John Jr., Paul Trice, Michael Anderson, little Christopher Anderson and Ray Samuels ll. My god-brothers Rudy Brown, Mark, Ruben and Jerry Freeman.

"A man, who gives a penny to the poor, receives one blessing. But a man, who gives his heart to the poor, receives much, much more."

Acknowledgements

I would first and foremost give thanks to my Heavenly Father JAH and my Lord and Savior Yeshua for blessing me with this gift, that I may do Their will. To all the men who participated in this project. And to my mom, for her encouragement, her prayers and the love in Christ that she has shared with me that keeps me going, in pursuing my goals. May JAH bless you all and Yeshua keep you all.

All the stories are fictional. However, they may reflect on what you or someone you know, may be experiencing in life. Bible scriptures were taken from the King James Version of the Holy Bible printed by Thomas Nelson Inc. copyright 1979, 1982, 1994

"A Man's Cry for His Father"

By: S.G.A
Copyright 2015

"A Letter from A Loving Father"

My sons; I am Your Father. I knew the path that you would take in your lives before I created the heavens and the earth; the choices that you would make before I spoke every living creature into existence; your thoughts and your desires before I designed the hills and the valleys and all the bodies of water that surrounded the land. I know you My sons on the day that I place you into the wombs of your mothers; and the day that your mothers released from their wombs. I know every hair on your head and every being of your fiber. I am your Father, your Dad, your Creator, your God; and all that you have chosen to call Me. I know every thought and desire, whether they be righteous or unrighteous. I know you. And when you call upon Me through your prayers, and even through your anger, I hear them even before you speak them. So, My sons, My boys, I know you. I am your Father. But, take heed to what I am about to say to you at this very moment. For that which you do that is unrighteous, I will punish. And that which you do that is righteous in My name and in the name of My Son, I will bless you. Understand that I know that you will commit many sins during your life there on earth; sins of words, deeds and thoughts. Even before you commit them, I know you. But My Son has made a way for all of you. I know it's hard walking the righteous paths that I have set all of you on. Each and every day, you are challenged by life. You are tested and tempted by the enemy. But know this. It's not the sins of words, deeds and thoughts that I look for. It's your sincere words of forgiveness which I desire to hear coming from your hearts. You may and will fool many people, but it's your heart which I will look upon. My desire is that none of you, My sons, should perish. You have a choice in your lives. And those choices will decide your fate. Always remember and never forget that My Son died for you; all of you, in hopes that you will draw closer to Me. He has made the path to Me much easier and much brighter. So, through your troubles, your trials, your heartaches, your temptations, your anger and your deceitfulness, through your lies and all that you do that displeases Me, know that I am your Father and I am here for you. To forgive and to forget them all. All that you have to do is, with a sincere heart and spirit; call on Me through the name of My Son, Yeshua. For He hears you just as I do. He talks in your favor. He sits on My right-hand side speaking for those who are true in their hearts and in their spirits. I love you My sons. And I will be here waiting to hear from you and to answer your prayers.

My days are like a shadow that lengthens, and I wither away like grass. But You, O Lord, shall endure forever, and the remembrance of Your name to all generations. You will arise and have mercy on Zion; for the time to favor her. Yes, the servants take pleasure in her stones and show favor to her dust. So, the nations shall fear the name of the Lord and all the kings of the earth, Your glory. For the Lord shall build up Zion. He shall appear in His glory. He shall regard the prayer of the destitute and shall not despise their prayer. This will come, that a people yet to be created, may praise the Lord. For He looked down from the heights of His sanctuary. From heaven, the Lord viewed the earth, to hear the groaning of the prisoner, to release those appointed to death. To declare the name of the Lord in Zion and His praise in Jerusalem, when the peoples are gathered together and the kingdoms to serve the Lord. He weakened my strength in the way; He shortened my days. I said, "O my God, do not take me away in the midst of my days. Your years are throughout all generations. Of old, You laid the foundations of the earth; and the heavens are the work of Your hands. They will perish, but You will endure. Yes, they will grow old like a garment. Like a cloak, You will change them and they will be changed." But You are the same and Your years will have no end. The Children of Your servants will continue and their descendants will be established before You. For this is the day in which I long to see you Father, and Your glory will rein forever more.

All these are the beginning of sorrows. Then they will deliver you up to tribulation and kill you; and you will be hated by all nations for My name's sake. And then many will be offended; will betray one another and will hate one another. Then many false prophets will rise up and deceive many. And because lawlessness will abound, the love of many will grow cold. But he who endures to the end shall be saved. And this gospel of the Kingdom will be preached in all the world as a witness to all the nations and then the end will come. So, My son. Stand fast in your faith in Me and My Son. For I am here with you, even until the end.

          Your Father:

Dear Father; my Father;

Be gracious to me Father, according to your loving-kindness; according to the greatness of Your compassion; blot out my transgressions; wash me thoroughly from my iniquities and cleanse me from my sins. For I know my transgressions and my sins are ever before me. Against You, You only, I have sinned and done what was evil in Your sight; so that You are justified when You speak and blameless when You judge. Behold, I was brought forth in iniquity and in sin my mother conceived me. Behold, You desire truth in the inward parts, and in the hidden part You will make me to know wisdom. Purge me with hyssop and I shall be clean; wash me and I shall be whiter than snow. Make me to hear joy and gladness; that the bones You have broken may rejoice. Hide Your face from my sins and blot out all my iniquities. Create in me a clean heart, O God, and renew a steadfast spirit within me. Do not cast me away from Your presence; and do not take Your Holy Spirit from me. Restore to me the joy of Your generous Spirit. Then I will teach transgressors Your ways and sinners shall be converted to You. Deliver me from the guilt of bloodshed, O God; the God of my salvation and my tongue shall sing aloud of Your righteousness. O Lord, open up my lips and my mouth shall show forth Your praise. For You do not desire sacrifice, or else I would give it; You do not delight in burnt offerings. The sacrifices of You my Father are a broken spirit. A broken and contrite heart. These God, You will not despise. Do good in Your good pleasure to Zion. Build the walls of Jerusalem. Then You shall be pleased with the sacrifices of righteousness with burnt offerings and whole burnt offerings. Whatever I must do, Father, I will do in Your name.

Sincerely: Your child

For many years, I have watched over you. From the day that you were born; to becoming the fine young man that you are. I have seen you take the gifts which I have blessed you with and squandered them on things of this world that was totally unrighteous and displeasing to Me. I was there when you committed the crimes that put you in prison. I was there when you walked away from Me to worship another god. I was there when you lied on others just to obtain material wealth. I was there when you committed adultery and fornication. When you even lied to others about Me. Throughout your life, I was there watching and waiting. Waiting for you to get back on the path which I had placed you on from the beginning. And now that you are prospering in your wealth, you have finally called upon Me with a sincere heart; with your face to the ground, seeking forgiveness for all that you have done wrong in your life and in My sight. And by that, I say to you, "Be of good cheer; your sins are forgiven you. Answer this question for Me from your heart. For which is easier to say, "Your sins are forgiven you or to arise and walk?" But that you may know that the Son of man has power on earth to forgive sins. Do not answer this question with words from your mouth but from within your heart and your spirit. So, My son, arise and go your way. For I have cleansed you of your unrighteousness. Know that I am the light of the world. He who follows Me shall not walk in darkness but have the light of life. I am proud of you My son, My child. Now go in Peace.

your **Father**

Father;

When I cry out to You, then my enemies will turn back. This I know, because You, Father are for me. In You my Father, I will praise Your word. In You my Lord and Savior, I have put my trust. I will not be afraid any more of the future nor the past. What can man do to me that I haven't already done to myself O Lord. Vows made to You my Lord, my God, are binding upon me; I will render praises to You; for You have delivered my soul from death. You have delivered my soul from the pits of hell. You have delivered my soul from an everlasting torment. Have You not kept my feet from falling, that I may walk before You O Father God in the light of the living?

With all that You have done for me in my entire existence on this earth, I extol You O Lord, for You have lifted me up and have not let my enemies rejoice over me. Yeshua my Lord, I cried out to You for help and You healed me. I will let the people know of Your mercy and Your grace, that they may call on You, O Lord, in their time of need, as You have with me. O thank You Father.

My son;
You truly have no need to fear man. What more can he do to you that wasn't done to My Son? When My

Son hung there on that tree dying, beaten, scorned and humiliated by His own people, He cried out to Me asking that I forgive them for what they have done, for they know not what they were doing. His only fear of rejection was when I had to turn away from Him when He took the sins of the world upon Himself. I had to, for no sin can be in My presence. My spirit cried out for My Son. And now at this moment, you, My child, has called out to Me with your tears and your fears. Do not be afraid My son, of those who will kill the body and have no more that they can do to you. But I will show you whom you should fear. Fear Him who, after He was killed, has power to cast into hell. Yes, I say to you My son, fear Him. Are not five sparrows sold for two copper coins; and not one of them is forgotten before God your Father? But the very hairs of your head are all numbered. Do not fear therefore; you are of more value than many sparrows. I need you to understand what I am saying to you. Also, I say to you, "Whoever confesses Me before men, the Son of man also will confess before the angels of God your Father. And anyone who speaks a word against the Son of man, it will be forgiven him. But to him who blasphemes against the Holy Spirit, it will not be forgiven. Now when they bring you to the synagogues and magistrates and authorities, and they will, do not worry about how or what you should answer or what you should say. Do you understand My son? Now, stop your weeping; get up off the ground For the Holy Spirit will teach you in that very hour what you ought to say." For I, your heavenly Father has not given you a spirit of fear; but of power and of love and of a sound mind.; brush yourself off and move forward in My name and in the name of My Son Yeshua.

I love you My son, My child

You shall have all the nations in derision. I will wait for You my Father. For You are my defense. My Father God of mercy shall come to meet me. You, my Father God shall let me see my desire on my enemies. Do not slay them, lest my people forget. Scatter them by Your power and bring them down, O Lord our shield, my shield. For the sins of their mouth and the words of their lips, let them even be taken in their pride. And for the cursing and the lying which they speak, consume them in wrath; consume them that they may not be. And let them know that God rules in Jacob to the end of the earth. Se'lah. And at evening, they return; they growl like a dog and go all around the city. They wander up and down for food and howl, if they are not satisfied. But I will sing of Your power. Yes, I will sing aloud of Your mercy in the morning. For You have been my defense and refuge in the day of my trouble. To You my Father, O my Strength, I will sing praises. For You, Father God is my defense. You are my only, my one and only Father in whom I love. My God of mercy.

I Love You Dad

Dear son;

I have taught you many things in your life as a child to prepare you for the world that you were about to enter. I taught you the difference between right and wrong, and the results of each decision that you make. And even though you chose to follow the world many times, I was still there for you; guiding you and protecting you every step of the way. Now that you are in prison for all the wrongs you have done, I am still with you. You are My child, My son and I will never leave your side; even though you have left Mine. Do you remember when you were 18 years old and you were running from the police and rival gangs out trying to kill you? I told you that you will reap what you sow. If you reap a righteous seed, you will sow a plentiful harvest. But if you reap an unrighteous seed, that you will sow nothing but a harvest of pain and sorrow; and sooner or later you will die in your sins. No one can serve two masters. For either he will hate the one and love the other or else he will be loyal to the one and despise the other. You cannot serve God your Father and mammon. Therefore, I say to you, "Do not worry about your life, what you will eat or what you will drink; nor about your body, what you will put on. Is not life more than food and the body more than clothes?" You know that I will never lead you down the wrong path. You know this. Look at the birds of the air; for they neither sow nor reap nor gather into barns; yet your Heavenly Father feeds them. Are you not more value than they? Which one of you by worrying can add one cubit to his stature? So why do you worry about clothing, food or even your life? I have all things in My power and in My hands. Now, as for those in whom you worship; you must make a choice. It would either be them (man) or Me, your Father. You cannot worship us both. It's your choice. It has always been your choice. I believe in you My son that you will make the right decision for your life.

I love you My son:

My Father

I call on You and You alone. For there is none like You, nor will there ever be; For You are great and do wondrous things. You alone are God my Father, my Dad. Teach me Your way, O Lord, my Father and I will walk in Your truth. Unite my heart to fear Your name. I will praise You O Lord my Father, my God, with all my heart and I will glorify Your name forevermore. For great is Your mercy toward me. and You Father have delivered my soul from the depths of She'ol. O God my Father the proud have risen against me and a mob of violent men have sought my life and have not set You before them. But You O Lord, are a good and righteous God; full of compassion and gracious longsuffering and abundant in mercy and truth. Oh, turn to me and have mercy on me. Give Your strength to Your servant and save the son of Your maidservant. Show me a sign for good, that those who hate me may see it and be ashamed. Because of You, oh Lord, have helped me and comforted me. Thank You for being my Father, my Dad, my God.

Love;
Your child

My son;

From the very first day that I breathed life into your tiny little body, you have always been My child whom I have saw favor. And as you grew into your teen years, you were ever so eager to learn more about Me. You have had your moments in those years that you found yourself in some uncompromising situations. However, you found the strength to overcome them with prayer and your trust in Me. And as a young man, I have seen you struggle with the temptations of the world. You even went as far as to act many of those temptations out. However, you diligently sought My forgiveness. As an adult, you have struggled with the world and all of its wealth. Yet, you chose to stay obedient. And because of your obedience, the world came after your soul to destroy it; to show you that you are truly unworthy of My love and My blessings. I hear your cry My son; and My ear is ever so close to you. That soft-spoken voice that you hear is I, your Father, reassuring you that everything is going to be alright. Now, let Me leave you with these words spoken from My Son to His Disciples and the many who desired to hear Him speak. And know that I love you and I am your Father. "Blessed are the poor in heart, for they shall see God. Blessed are the poor in spirit, for theirs is the kingdom of heaven. Blessed are the meek, for they shall inherit the earth. Blessed are those who hunger and thirst after righteousness, for they shall be filled. Blessed are the merciful, for they shall obtain mercy. Blessed are those who are persecuted for righteousness sake, for theirs is the kingdom of heaven." This one is for you personally, My son. "Blessed are you, when they revile and persecute you and say all kinds of evil against you falsely for My sake." Remember My child, that you are the salt of the earth; but if the salt loses its flavor, how shall it be seasoned? It is then good for nothing but to be thrown out and trampled underfoot by men. With

My Son by your side and in your heart, you are the light of the world. A city that is on a hill cannot be hidden. So, My child, My son; let your light so shine before men, that they may see your good works and glorify your Father in heaven. Keep on shining My son. Keep on shining.

Love;
Your Father

Father:
Because zeal for Your house has eaten me up, and the reproached of those who reproach You have fallen to me. When I wept and chastened my soul with fasting, that became my reproach. I also made sackcloth my garment. I became a byword to them. those who sit in the gate speak against me and I am the song of drunkards. But as for me, my prayer is to You O Lord; in the acceptable time. O God, my Father, in the multitude of Your mercy, hear me in the truth of Your salvation. Deliver me out of the mire and let me not sink. Let me be delivered from those who hate me and out of the deep waters, let not the floodwaters overflow me, nor let the deep swallow me up. And let not the pit shut its mouth on

me. Hear me O Lord; for Your loving-kindness is good. Turn to me according to the multitude of Your tender mercies, and do not hide Your face from Your servant, for I am in trouble. Hear me speedily. Draw near to my soul and redeem it. Deliver me because of my enemies. You know my reproach, my shame and my dishonor. My adversaries are all before You. My reproach has broken my heart and I am full of heaviness. I looked for someone to take pity, but there was none; and for comforters, but I found none. They also gave me gall for my food and for my thirst they gave me vinegar to drink. Let their table become a snare before them and their well-being a trap. Let their eyes be darkened, so that they do not see and make their loins shake continually. Pour out Your indignation upon them and let Your wrathful anger take hold of them. Let their dwelling place be desolate. Let no one live in their tents. For they persecute the ones You have struck and talk of grief of those You have wounded. Add iniquity to their iniquity and let them not cone into Your righteousness. Let them be blotted out of the Book of the Living and not be written with the righteous. But I am poor and sorrowful. Let Your salvation, O Father God, set me up on high. I will praise the name of God; You my Father, with a song and will magnify You with thanksgiving. This also shall please You my Father, my Lord, better than an ox or bull, which has horns and hooves. The humble shall see this and be glad. And for those who see You Father God, their hearts shall live. I will tell them all, "For the Lord hears the poor and does not despise His prisoners. Let heaven and earth praise Him; the seas and everything that moves in them. For God will save Zion and build the cities of Judah, that they may dwell there and possess it. Also, the descendants of His servants shall inherit it, and those who love His name shall dwell in it." I will go and tell them.

Thank You Father;
    Your child

Dear son;
Don't ever feel within your heart and spirit that
I am not aware of what you are going through. For

I am aware of all things that are happening to My children. Especially to those who have chosen to follow in My way and stay obedient to My word. You have gone this far in your journey with My Son; continue on with Him. And in your continued journey, you will be betrayed even by your parents and brothers, relatives and friends alike; you are not alone. And they will put some of you to death. And you My son, will be hated by all for My name's sake. But not a hair of your head shall be lost. By your patience, possess your soul. And as much as it hurts your heart to see your own family and your closest friends turn against you, you must wait on Me. No tears of sorrow nor pain shall you exhibit. You are My son, in whom I am proud of. I have prayed for you that your faith should not fail; and when you have returned to Me, strengthen your brethren, your sisters, your parents and relatives and even your closest friends. Do this My son and know this, "Who is greater; he who sits at the table or he who serves?

Is it not he who sits at the table? Yet, I am among you as the One who serves.

Your Father

My Lord;

The proud have hidden a snare for me and cords. They have spread a net by the wayside. They have set traps for me O Father. I would say to You,

"You are my God. Hear the voice of my supplications, O Lord. You are the strength of my salvation. You have covered my head in the day of battle. Do not grant, O Lord, my Father, the desires of the wicked. Do not further his wicked scheme; lest they be exalted. Se'lah: As for the head of those who surround me, let the evil of their lips cover them. Let burning coals fall upon them. Let them be cast into the fire. Into deep pits, that they rise not up again. Let not a slanderer be established in the earth. Let the evil hunt the violent man to overthrow him." I know that the Lord will maintain the cause of the afflicted and justice for the poor. Surely the righteous shall give thanks to Your name O Father in heaven. The upright shall dwell in Your presence. With all that is within my heart, soul, mind and spirit, I truly give thanks to You, my Father, my Dad, my God.

Your son:

My son;

For years, I have watched as you travelled to worship service every Sunday confessing your sins to your priest. I have seen you bow to your knees in front of a statue of the Virgin Mary. By the way, that was the only time that I chose her to bare my Son. After which, she had other children by her earthly husband Joseph. Yet, you chose to bow to her to pray for peace within your home and your family. I've heard your prayers to the saints asking to bring you prosperity in your life. Even though you may have ended your prayer in the name of My Son and I, you still wondered why your prayers were not answered. Well My son, let Me tell you why. First and foremost, I am a jealous Father. And that no one can come to Me except by My Son, Yeshua. Now, sit and listen as I teach you again on how you should pray. And when you pray, you shall not be like the hypocrites. For they love to pray standing in the synagogues and on the corners of the streets, that they may be seen by men. Assuredly, I say to you; they have their reward. But you My son, when you pray go into your room, and when you have shut the door, pray to Me your Father, who sees in secret will reward you openly; and when you pray do not use vain repetitions as the heathens do. For they think that they will be heard for their many words. Therefore, My son, do not be like them. For I, your Father knows the things you have need of before you ask Me. In this manner, therefore pray, "Our Father in heaven. Hallowed be Your name, Your kingdom come. Your will be done on earth as it is in heaven. Give us this day our daily bread and forgive us our debts as we forgive our debtors. And lead us not into temptation but deliver us from the evil one. For Yours is the kingdom and the power and the glory forever. Amen." So, you see My son, that's all you have to pray to Me and your prayers will be answered. Now go among your family, your wife and children and your friends; even your enemies and share this prayer with them. Teach them and place it in their hearts and spirit. Especially your children that they may teach their children and their children's children; that the generations after you have left this world, may truly know how to pray to

Me with truth and with honor and in spirit. Now go My son with all My blessings. And with you I will send My Holy Spirit, to guide you and to teach you so much more.

Love, your Father

Father;

Do not let me eat of their delicacies. Let the righteous strike me. It shall be a kindness. And let him rebuke me. It shall be as excellent as oil. Let my head not refuse it. For, still my prayer is against the deeds of the wicked. Their judges are overthrown by the sides of the cliffs, and they hear my words; for they are sweet. Our bones are scattered at the mouth of the grave, as when one plows and breaks up the earth. But my eyes are upon You O God my Father. In You I take refuge. Do not leave my soul destitute. Keep me from the snares they have laid for me and from the traps of the workers of iniquity. Let the wicked fall into their own nets while I escape safety. Only You Father can guide me through these troubling times and in You I will seek protection and safety. I love You my Father.

Son;

You have sought My help for many years. I have blessed you with prosperity. I have enlarged your territory. Increased your household and have blessed each and every one of your children in the same manner. But yet you still cry out to Me. You have taken that in which I have blessed you with and squandered it on all manners of worldly desires. Before your blessings came upon you, you were as humble and content with your life as a child. Now, as a man, I have seen what has become of you. I am highly displeased. You have placed judgment on those who are less fortunate than you are. You take your possessions and you hide them from thieves and robbers, instead of sharing your blessings with those who are poor. I did not teach you these ways. Neither did My Son Yeshua. And now that men have come to rob and steal from you and your family, you cry out to Me to discipline them all. I will not. For I have told you before to not lay up for yourself treasures on earth, where moth and rust destroy, and where thieves break in and steal. But lay up for yourself treasures in heaven where neither moth nor rust destroys and where thieves do not break in and steal. For where your treasure is, there your heart will be also. I have also taught you that you judge not, that you be judged. For with what judgment you judge, you will be judged; and with measure you use, it will be measured back to you. Why do you look at the speck in your brother's eye, but do not consider the plank in your own eye? Or how can you say, "Let me remove the speck from your eye," and look, a plank is in your own eye. You know My son what that makes you, right; a hypocrite. You must first remove the plank from your own eye, and then you will see clearly to remove the speck from your brother's eye. Clean out your own closet first My son, that your children may see My Son in you. Because right now, your children see no part of Me nor My Son Yeshua in you. You know what must be done. Now do it. But do it in My name and in the name of the One who sacrificed His life for you. I still love you My son, My child. I want only the best for you and your children and your entire family. And if I didn't love you, I would not chastise you. So, get up off the ground, brush the dirt off your clothes and stop your whining and get back on the path in which I put you on.

Love: Your Father

My Lord, my Savior;

I know You have heard when I called on You. I have also told them, "to be angry but not to sin; and to meditate within your heart on your bed and be still. Offer the sacrifices of righteousness and put your trust in the Lord." Oh, Father in heaven, there are many who say, "Who will show us any good?" Lord, lift up the light of Your countenance upon us. You have put gladness in my heart more than in the season that their grain and wine increased. I will both lie down in peace and sleep. For You alone, O Lord make me dwell in safety. So please my Father, my God, as I pray to You right now and give ear to my words. Consider my meditation. Give heed to the voice of my cry, my King and my God. For to You and You alone will I pray. My voice You shall hear in the morning O Lord. In the morning I will direct it to You and I will look up. For You are not a God who takes pleasure in wickedness, nor shall evil dwell with You. The boastful shall not stand in Your sight. You hate all workers of iniquity. You shall destroy those who speak falsehood. For You my Father, abhors the bloodthirsty and deceitful man. But as for I, Father, I will come into Your house in the multitude of Your mercy. In fear of You I will worship toward Your Holy Temple. Please Father, in the name of Yeshua, lead me in Your righteousness because of my enemies. Make Your way straight before my face; For there is no faithfulness in their mouth. Their inward part is destruction. Their throat is an open tomb. They flatter with their tongue. Pronounce them guilty, O God, my Father. Let them fall by their own counsels. Cast them out in the multitude of their transgressions. For they have rebelled against You. But let all those rejoice who put their trust in You. Let them ever shout out for joy, because You defend them. Let those also who love Your name be joyful in You. For You my Father, my Dad, will bless the righteous; with favor You will surround him as with a shield. You are my Father in whom I love so much… Your son;

My dearest child;

You have continuously walked in the way of My counsel. You have kept My commandments. You have given of your tithes and offerings as I have required of you to do. You kept yourself mindful of My presence. You have given testimony to many people about My love, grace and mercy. You stayed humble when your enemies sought you out to bring harm upon you and your family. You were steadfast when many placed stumbling blocks in your path. You even fasted and prayer for those who placed you in prison for no reason. And you are still fasting and praying while I continue to bless you. You have remained obedient to My counsel and I am proud of you. Now it's time for you to go on a journey. A journey to a place where My children has forgotten all about Me and about My Son Yeshua; A place among your own people, where idol worshipping is even among the little ones. Where at one time they called out to Me to deliver them from their oppressors, as did My children during the time of Moses. And you will see among them as they commit all manner of sin just as My people did when I freed them out of the hands of the Pharaohs. You will see woman with woman and man with man. You will see the death of many of My little ones. Murder will be out of control. Robbery and theft are running ramped. There's no fear of Me nor of death among your people. It will not be an easy task for you. Many will hate you for what you are about to say and do. Some may even try to take your life. But know this My son, your life belongs to Me. And it is I who decides life or death over My children. So, as you go to prepare yourself for this journey, I am going to equip you with My own preparation which is My word. Brand these words into your heart and into your mind. First: Beware of false prophets, who come to you in sheep's clothing; but inwardly they are ravenous wolves. You will know them by their fruits. Second: Do men gather grapes from thorn bushes or figs from thistles? Even so, every good tree bears good fruit, but a bad tree bears bad fruit. A good tree cannot bear bad fruit, nor can a bad tree bear good fruit. Every tree that does not bear good fruit is cut down and thrown into the fire. Therefore, by their fruits you will know them. You are going to find yourself at times very angry by My children's ways. But you, My son, must stay strong in My word. There will be those who will hate Me and My Son. Try not to lose your temper, because I know that you can. Just do as I have instructed you to do and you will be just fine. The Helper will be with you every step of the way.

        Love; your Father

Father;
I have purposed that my mouth shall not transgress, concerning the works of men by the words of Your lips. I have kept away from the paths of the

destroyer. Uphold my steps dear Father in Your paths, that my footsteps may not slip. I have called upon You, for You will hear me, O God of my fathers. Incline Your ear to me and hear my speech. Show Your marvelous loving-kindness by Your right hand, O You who save those who trust in You from those who rise up against them. Keep me my Father as the apple of Your eye. Hide me under the shadows of Your wings from the wicked who oppress me; from my deadly enemies who surround me. They have closed up their fat hearts; with their mouths they speak proudly. They have now surrounded us in our steps; they have set their eyes, crouching down to the earth as a lion is eager to tear his prey, and as a young lion lurking in secret places. Arise, O Lord my Father, my Dad; Please confront him; cast him down. Deliver my life from the wicked with Your sword; with Your hand, from men O Lord, from men of the world who have their portion in this life, and whose belly You fill with Your hidden treasure. They are satisfied with children and leave the rest of their possessions for their babies. As for me Father, I will see Your face in righteousness. I shall be satisfied when I awake in Your likeness.

          Thank You, my Lord

My son, My servant;

Oh, how humble you have become throughout your years. In the midst of your storm, you stayed humble. In the face of your adversities, you remained humble. You are standing strong and firm in your trust and your faith in Me. Even the angels here in heaven are rejoicing. And as My Son, Yeshua sits here on My right-hand side, He too is smiling upon you. You have come a long way in your life from whence you began. From an abusive earthly father, to prison, drug use, homelessness, worshipping idol gods. You have triumphed over your enemies with prayer and faith; with fasting and trust. And even now as your enemies come upon you and place stumbling blocks in your path to have you to fall, your faith and trust in My Son and I are awesome. You are slow to anger. But, when you do get angry, you do not sin. You have become the strong leader of your household. Your children now desire to follow in your footsteps; as does your grand-children. Your wife is honored to stand by your side. You have set an example for your generation and the generations to come, on how I am to be worshipped and honored in love, truth and spirit. And for your ever-loving faith and trust in Me, I have a task in which I trust you will fulfill. Go therefore and make disciples of all nations, baptizing them in the name of your Father, His Son and in the Holy Spirit; teaching them to observe all things that I have commanded you. And lo, I am with you always; even to the end of the age. I love you My son.

Remember, my Lord, my Father, my Dad, Your tender-mercies and Your loving-kindness; for they are from old. Please do not remember the sins of my youth nor my transgressions; according to Your mercy, remember m for Your goodness' sake, O Lord. I would tell everyone, "Good and upright is the Lord, my Father. Therefore, He teaches sinners in the way. The humble He guides in justice." This is who You are Father. I know, because You have done this for me. I would also tell them that, " The humble, He teaches His way and all the paths of the Lord are mercy and truth. Too such as keep His covenant and His testimonies." For Your name's sake my Father, my Lord, my God, pardon my iniquity, for it is great. Please Father, I beg of You. Please turn Yourself to me and have mercy on me; For I am desolate and afflicted. The troubles of my heart have enlarged. Bring me out of my distresses. Look on my affliction and pain and forgive all my sins. Consider my enemies, for they are many and they hate me with cruel hatred. Keep my soul and deliver me, Dad. Let me not be ashamed; for I put my trust in You. Let integrity and uprightness preserve me. For I will wait for You, my Father, my Dad.

I love You my Lord:
Your son

Before your mother conceived you, I had a plan already set for your life. You may not remember much of your childhood, but I do, all of it. When you were born deathly ill and Lucifer tried to take you

from Me, I said, "Not this child." When the doctors gave up on you. But I didn't. Seeing your small and fragile little body, fighting to stay alive as your mother, grandmother and aunt all stayed in very close contact with Me through their prayers. I was there watching you grow up with many more physical and medical complications. Watching you go through even more surgeries to your very young body, all done to keep you alive. I was there in your young years watching you fight the rejection you received from your peers in school and in the community where you lived. I was there when you fought to achieve many goals in your young teen years, just to watch them fade away, due to the constant words told to you that, "You will never amount to anything in life because you're worthless." I was there when you fought for the love of the man who raised you, in order that you can feel whole as to say that you have a father, only to be beat and abused by him and never hearing the words," I love you son." I was there when you stood up to this same man when he tried to harm your mother. I was there when you went off to the military, only to be rejected by them. I was there when you disobeyed the laws of the land; and because of your irresponsibility, it put you in prison. While there, you fought to stay alive and to survive and be accepted. You fought so very hard to keep many unhealthy relationships alive, in order that you would never be left alone and by yourself. You fought with the pain of knowing that when you became a man that you will never know the true meaning of fatherhood. Then you fought ever so hard in believing that you were worthless and no good to anyone; even Myself. You have fought, and fought, and fought. And you are still fighting with yourself. You have been fighting all your life My child. You even try to fight for the respect and honor for Me and My Son, Yeshua, in which you really don't need to. For My Son have fought and won, not only the battle, but the war. But now there is another war brewing as I speak to you now and has been brewing for a very long time. This war is for the souls of all mankind. My sons and daughters are falling so far away from Me, that My spirit cries out to them. And My little ones are dying at an alarming rate. Continue the work in which I have blessed you with. You are My son, My child. And you have found a righteous war to fight and I will give you the tools to fight it, which is My Holy Spirit. You are My fighting son. That's who you are, a fighter. You've come a long way from whence you began. It wasn't easy, but you are still moving forward. And you're moving forward in My name and in the name of My Son. I am with you every step of the way. Continue on in your work and you will see the fruits of your labor. I am with you, even til the end of time and beyond.

Love: your Father

Father;

You have said in Your word that You will repay my enemies. I have told many of my friends that You will repay my enemies for their evil; cut them off in Your truth. As for me, I will freely sacrifice to You. I will praise Your name. O Lord, my Father for You are good. Just the other night, I called my brother Eddie and told him how You have delivered me out of all my troubles, and my eyes has seen its desire upon my enemies." So, I am asking of You my Father, give ear to my prayer, O God and do not hide Yourself from my supplication. Attend to me and hear me. I am restless in my complaint and moan noisily because of the voice of the enemy, because of the oppression of the wicked; for they bring down trouble upon me and in wrath they hate me. My heart is severely pained within me and the terrors of death have fallen upon me. Fearfulness and trembling have come upon me. And horror has overwhelmed me. So, I say, "Oh, that I had wings like a dove! I would fly away and be at rest. Indeed Father, I would wander far off and remain in the wilderness. I would hasten my escape from the windy storm and tempest." Oh, my Father, my Lord, destroy and divide their tongues. For I have seen violence and strife in the city. Day and night, they go around on its walls. It hurts my spirit Father that iniquity and trouble are also in the midst of it. As I walk through the city, I can see destruction in its midst. Oppression and deceit do not depart from the streets. For it is not an enemy who reproaches me; then I can bear it. Nor is it one who hates me, who has exalted himself against me; then I could hide from him. But it was a man, my equal, my companion and my acquaintance. We took street counsel together and walked to the house of God in the throng. I wish no harm to anyone. Your judgment is true. Let death seize them. Let them go down alive into hell. For wickedness is in their dwellings and among them. As for myself Father, I will call upon You my Lord, my God, and You shall save me. Evening and morning and at noon, I will pray and cry aloud, and Your Son Yeshua, He shall hear my voice; for He has redeemed my soul in peace from the battle that was against me; for there were many against me. I know that You, my Father, my God, will hear and afflict them, because they do not change. Therefore, they do not fear You. They have put forth their hands against those who were at peace with them. They have broken their covenant. The words of their mouth were smoother than butter. But war was in their heart. Their words were drawn swords. I told them to cast their burdens on You Father and You shall sustain them. They will never permit the righteous to be moved. But You, my Father God, my Dad, shall bring them down to the pit of destruction. Bloodthirsty and deceitful men shall not live out half their days. I will trust in You and only You, my Father, my Dad.

I love You

You have been running and hiding for such a long time from those you have called friend. From those who have been trying to take your life. But let Me assure you My son; I alone have the power to give life and the power to take it. I am aware of all of your

troubles, so you need not worry your heart nor your spirit of what anyone can do to you. Listen and learn My child. Behold, a sower went out to sow, and as he sowed, some seed fell by the wayside; and the birds came and devoured them. Some seed fell on stony places, where they did not have much earth; and they immediately sprang up because they had no depth of earth. But when the sun was up, they were scorched, and because they had no roots they withered away. And some fell among thorns, and the thorns sprang up and choked them. But others fell on good ground and yielded a crop; some a hundredfold, some sixty, some thirty. He, who has ears to hear, let him listen. You may not quite understand what I am saying to you. So, I am going to explain it to you in this manner. "When anyone hears and listens to the Word of the kingdom, and does not understand it, then the wicked one comes and snatches away what was sown in his heart. This is he who received seed by the wayside. But he received the seed on the stony places, this is he who hears the Word and immediately receives it with joy, yet he has no roots in himself, but endures only for a while. For when tribulation or persecution arises because of the Word, immediately he stumbles. Now, he who received seed among the thorns is he who hears the word and the cares of this world and the deceitfulness of riches choke the Word, and he becomes unfruitful. But he who received seed on good ground is he who not only hears the Word, but listens and understand it, who indeed bears fruit and produce; some a hundredfold, some sixty, some thirty." Now do you understand My son? So, worry not for what men, let alone anyone else can do to you. I have great works for you to do. It's going to be alright. You have trusted in Me all your life, now continue to trust in Me to the end. Love; your Father

p.s. The field is the world; the good seeds are the sons of the kingdom, but the tares are the sons of the wicked one. You My son, are that good seed.

Father;

You have heard my supplications. For You, my Father, will receive my prayer. Please Lord, let all my enemies be ashamed and greatly troubled. Let them turn back and be ashamed suddenly. My Father, in You I put my trust. Save me from all those who persecute me and deliver me, lest they tear me like a lion, rendering me in pieces, while there is none to deliver. O Lord, my God, if I have done this, if there is iniquity in my hands; if I have repaid evil to him who was at peace with me or have plundered my enemy without cause; if I have done such things Father, then let my enemy pursue me and overtake me. Yes, let him trample my life to the earth and lay my honor in the dust. Arise, O Lord, my Father, in Your anger, lift Yourself up because of the rage of my enemies. Please Father, in the name of Yeshua, rise up for me to the judgment You have commanded, so the congregation of the peoples shall surround You; for their sakes, therefore, return on high. It's You my Father, my Lord, shall judge the people. As for myself oh Lord, judge me according to my righteousness and according to my integrity within me. With tears in my eyes and a sincere heart and spirit, Father, O my Father God, let the wickedness of the wicked come to an end, but establish the just. For the righteous, my Lord, You tests the hearts and minds of all. My defense is of You, who saves the upright in heart. I know that You are a just judge. And that You are angry with the wicked every day. One night, I was at a friend's home; a friend who was lost to the world. As we sat and talked, he started to cry because he was so lost in the world, that he wasn't sure if he wanted to return back to You or not. He was afraid that if he returned to You, he would lose all that he worked so hard for. I told him what would happen if he didn't return back to You. I told him that You will sharpen Your sword; You bend Your bow and make it ready. You also prepared for Yourself instruments of death. You make Your arrows into fiery shafts and behold the wicked brings forth iniquity. And the wicked brings forth trouble and falsehood. He has made a pit and dug it out and had fallen into the ditch which he made and that his trouble shall return upon his own head. His violent dealings shall come down on his own crown." Then I said to him, "My brother, I will praise the Lord according to His righteousness and will sing praise to the name of the Lord Most High." With tears in his eyes Father, he asked me to help him return back to You. Deliver him Father in the Holy name of Yeshua, who is my Lord and Savior, and Your Son. Thank You Father for Your love and for returning a lost child back to You.

I love You: Your son

You have endured so much pain and sorrow. I am here for you My child, my son; For many have falsely accused you of many unrighteous deeds. The charitable deeds that you have done and still continue to do, they curse and mock you for them. Remember My son, I am your Father, your Creator, and I see all. I know of all that you have done to help those that are less fortunate than you are. From working in the shelters to visiting the sick in the hospitals. Even to the giving of your finances to help the needy. I know all; for I am God; your Father. Do you remember when you came to Me with your prayer concerning the issue of giving, and the answer that I gave you? Let Me remind you of that answer. Therefore, when you do charitable deeds, do not sound a trumpet before you, as the hypocrites do in the synagogues and in the streets, that they may have glory from men. Assuredly, I say to you, "They have their reward." But when you do a charitable deed, do not let your left hand know what your right hand is doing, that your charitable deed may be in secret and your Father who sees in secret will Himself reward you openly." Many will hate you and be jealous and envious of you because of what you do in My name and in the name of My Son, Yeshua. Even those in whom I have blessed will despise you. They will slander you and say all manner of evil against you. So, you stand fast My son and hold strong to My Word and I will see you through those troubling times. I promise you this. And as your Father, I have never broken a promise to none of My children. Not one. Be strong My son and stand in your faith.... **Your Father**

My sons; I, your Father, your Creator, am so very proud of you. You have fought the good fight and have prevailed. You have finished the race and never gave up. You have kept your faith in Me and in My

Son. So, I say unto you my child, "Well done My good and faithful servant. You have been faithful over a few things; I will now make you a ruler over many. Well done my son. Well done.

A good man draws a circle around himself and cares for those within; his wife and his children. Other men draw a larger circle and brings with them their brothers and sisters. And some men have a greater destiny which is designed by God. They must draw around themselves a circle that includes many, many more.

A war is raging in the hearts of every man. A war between good and evil. Which one wins? The one we feed the most

How long, O Lord? Will You hide Yourself forever? Will Your wrath burn like fire? Remember what my span of life is, please.

Message from a Very Wise Man

My brothers;

When I speak of my brothers; I speak of every man that walks on the face of the earth; every man of every culture, of every religious belief, of every race. During my time, life was different; our ways were different; our cultures were different. However, there is one thing that has never changed throughout the history of mankind; and that is the words and knowledge of our beloved teacher; our heavenly Father and Creator, the Most High God and His Beloved Son, Yeshua. Just as He taught me during my time, He still teaches His word in your time. Yes, some of the words may have changed due to the different languages and cultures of people throughout the centuries, however, His word has never changed. We all were given the gift of life, that we may be fruitful and multiply and replenish this place we call home, earth; for His glory and His honor. Granted, some things may not have gone as planned, but we as men of God, all men, have an obligation to our families, our friends, our loved ones, ourselves, even to our enemies, to uphold the truth and the wisdom that has been passed down since the beginning of time. For, the wisdom and the knowledge of the Most High God is the only thing that can bring you out and see you through the troubles and hardships in which you are about to experience; troubles that I have never seen in my entire life here on earth, but have been told about. Now, I am aware that in your century, there is street wisdom and street knowledge, which you may or have used in order to survive. But your purpose my brothers is to teach the people of God's wisdom and discipline; to help them understand the insight of the wise; to teach them to live disciplined and successful lives; to help them do what is right, just and fair.; to give insight to the simple, and to give knowledge and discernment to the young. Understand this my brothers, that the fear of the Lord is the foundation of true knowledge. And know that the foolish ones despise wisdom and discipline. My brothers; never forget the teachings that your heavenly Father have taught you and store them within your heart and soul. If you do this, you will live many years and your life will be satisfied. Never, by no means, let loyalty and kindness leave you. Take them in your hands and tie them around your neck as a reminder. Write them down deep within your heart; then you will find favor with both the Most High God and the people that surround you each and every day, and you will earn a good reputation. Trust in the

Lord my brothers with all your heart and lean not to your own understanding. Seek your Father's will in all that you do, and He will show you which path to take in your lives. Don't be impressed with your street wisdom and knowledge but fear the Lord and turn away from that which is evil and not of your Father nor your Savior. Whatever you do to make a living, honor Him with your wealth and with the best part of everything you produce from it; then He will fill your home with plenty. Brothers, please don't reject your Father's discipline and don't be upset when He corrects you; for He corrects those He loves, just as an earthly father corrects his child in whom he delights. I know that this world can lay heavy on one's heart and spirit. But you must, by any means necessary, stay focused on Yeshua and don't lose sight of common sense and discernment; for they will refresh your soul. By holding tight and staying focused to common sense and discernment, they will keep you safe on your way and your feet will not stumble. You can even go to bed at night without fear and lie down and sleep soundly; for the Lord is your security. He will keep your feet from being caught in a trap. He has done this for me many times over in my life. And when I say many times over; believe me when I say many, many times over. Do not withhold good from those who deserve it; when its in your power to help them. Many years ago, when I was just a young man, relaxing in my home, I received a message. A message that still lives within my heart and soul even as the very old man that I am today. I'm going to share that message with you. And it read. "Young man; I dwell with prudence and find out knowledge and discernment. For the fear of the Lord is to hate evil, pride and arrogance and the evil way. And a perverse mouth I hate. Counsel is mine and is sound wisdom. I am understanding and I have strength. By me, kings reign and rulers decree justice. By me, princes' rule and nobles, all the judges of the earth. I love those who love me; and those who seek me diligently, will find me; and if they so desire to look for me, riches and honor are with me; enduring riches and righteousness. My fruit is better than gold. Yes, than fine gold; and my revenue, than choice silver. I transverse the way of righteousness; in the midst of the path of justice, that I may cause those who love me to inherit wealth, that I may fill their treasures. The Lord possessed me in the beginning of His way; before His works of old. I have been established from everlasting; from the beginning, before there was ever an earth. When there were no depth, I was brought forth. When there were no fountains abounding with water; before the mountains were settled before the hills, I was brought forth. While as yet, your Father had not made the earth nor the fields, nor the primal dust of the world. Did you know, young man, that when your heavenly Father prepared the heavens,

I was there. When He drew a circle on the face of the deep; when your Father established the clouds above; when your Father strengthened the fountains of the deep; when your Father assigned to the sea, its limit, so that the waters would not transgress His command; when your Father marked out the foundations of the earth, then, I was beside Him as a master craftsman. And I was daily His delight, rejoicing always before Him, in His presence; rejoicing in His inhabited world. And my delight was with the sons of men. Now therefore, listen to me young man. For blessed are those who keep my ways, hear instructions and be wise, and do not disdain it. Blessed is the one who listens to me, watching daily at my gates, waiting at the posts of my doors. For whoever finds me finds life and obtains favor from the Most High God. But, know this too young man. That, he who sins against me, wrongs his own soul; all those who hate me, loves death. So, be mindful of my words and instructions, that your life may be fulfilled in the glory of your Father in heaven. I will always be with you; no matter where you are, no matter where you go. I will always be with you; guiding you through the steps of life. Sincerely, Wisdom." That message has kept me strong in my walk with my Father. And I wish to pass that same message on to all of you my brothers. Read it over and over again until it is burned within your hearts and minds. Let no one, man or woman, stray you from the path that your Father has placed you on. Well, I'm a little tired now. Its time for me to rest. But in closing, I leave you with this. Be mindful of your Father's presence. Know that all of you are the sons of the Most High God. Follow His instructions and you can't go wrong and may the Lord bless you; may the Lord keep you. May He shine His face upon you and be gracious to you. May He lift up His countenance upon you and keep you in perfect peace.

Your brother: Solomon

From the Author

We were created in our Father's image; in the likeness of His image. However, we do not carry ourselves in respect of that image. We are aware that there are other forces involved that will prevent us from doing so. But that does not give us the right to destroy the lives of others and even ourselves. If man is willing to fight for their countries, their families, their planet, their right to exists, then why wouldn't man fight for the position they once held in the beginning. The position of being God's first born. We are His first born: his first living, breathing soul. That is a status of excellence, of honor and of love; a status that is not to be taken lightly; a status that carries a lot of responsibility; a status that does not make us better than anyone else; a status that does not make us better than any woman. It is a status of honor, respect, loyalty, trust and love to our heavenly Father and to the women that He has placed in our lives. As I said earlier; There are other forces involved that will try to prevent us from doing God's will. Forces that we cannot fight alone. That is why God, our Father sent His Son, Yeshua, to help us and deliver us by giving us the spiritual weapons to fight. For those weapons are not meant for us to fight each other, but the spiritual wickedness in high places. That is why He speaks to us about putting on the whole amour of God. That we may be able to stand in the evil day. We are men of God. Every one of us. From Christian to Muslim; from Hindu to Catholic. From every living, breathing religious man on this planet. No matter what you may believe, we are still His first born. You can deny it, but you can't escape the reality of it. So, I say to all men alike; whether be black or white; Hispanic or Asian; put aside your religious and cultural differences and take back that which was gifted to you from the beginning. The true gift of life. Let our women and our children of our lands see the trueness of God in each and every one of us. Not as males, but as men of the Most High God.

Thank you for reading "Heart of The Spirit" volume #2. May JAH bless you and Yeshua keep you. May He shine His face upon you and be gracious to you. May He lift up His countenance upon you and keep you in perfect peace S.G.A.

My Personal Monthly Journal

After this page, you will find an open monthly journal where you may write down your own spiritual prayers and thoughts. Most people think that only women keep journals. But that's not true. There are men who do have a journal. Some journals express your thoughts and feelings towards a person or a situation. This journal is between you and your Creator, which makes it extremely personal. There are men who desire to express themselves emotionally and spiritually but feel that they are unable to. If a man cannot express himself vocally, then hopefully he can express himself in writing. There are twelve pages, starting with January to December. Please use them as you see fit. And again, I thank you.

January

February

March

April

May

June

July

August

September

October

November

December

HEART OF THE SPIRIT

Made in the USA
Columbia, SC
21 September 2020